"This Snow's If We're Going Back Into Town, We Need To Go Now."

"My cabin's a short drive from here," he said. "Don't know about you, but I'd rather dance naked in that snow than be stuck in a cab when she wakes up crying."

The baby squeaked again, louder this time. Then her nose wrinkled before she settled fitfully. Trinity pressed her lips together for a moment before her hold on the seat belt eased.

"All right. We'll go to your place."

Wasting no time, Zack tapped the driver's shoulder and the cab pulled carefully out of the snow-clogged drive.

Despite her stand, instinct said she was as attracted to him as he was to her. Could be interesting getting to know her a little better.

Gazing out the window, Zack slowly smiled.

Who was he kidding? Truth was that he'd like to get to know Ms. Matthews, and her attitude, a whole lot more.

Dear Reader,

When my editor asked if I wanted to write another Billionaires and Babies book, my answer was an emphatic *You bet!* Nothing brings out a big strong man's vulnerabilities more than placing a tiny person in his uncompromising line of advance. And as I tossed around ideas for a story line, the ways to create and widen cracks in my hero's armor began to grow.

My favorite kind of hero is in charge of his environment. He knows what he wants and how to get it on his terms. I began to scheme ways to place as many roadblocks in cool-and-collected Zack Harrison's "environment" as possible. First, a much coveted business deal simply won't come together. Then a freak snowstorm leaves Zack isolated with a baby who has materialized out of thin air. Finally, there's an incredibly sexy woman who not only disapproves of practically everything Zack stands for, but also manages to challenge his deepest beliefs. *Check, check and check!*

After a single day and two amazing nights, when these problems are finally cleared from his life, Zack barely recognizes himself. This predicament—the unprecedented feelings Trinity Matthews and that abandoned baby brought out in him—it was all supposed to be *Strictly Temporary.*

Please visit my website, www.robyngrady.com, for the latest on contests, releases and to link up on Twitter and my Facebook page. Hope you enjoy the story!

Best wishes,

Robyn

ROBYN GRADY

STRICTLY TEMPORARY

HARLEQUIN®
entertain, enrich, inspire™

Recycling programs
for this product may
not exist in your area.

ISBN-13: 978-0-373-73182-4

STRICTLY TEMPORARY

Copyright © 2012 by Robyn Grady

www.Harlequin.com

Printed in U.S.A.

Books by Robyn Grady

Harlequin Desire

The Billionaire's Bedside Manner #2093
Millionaire Playboy, Maverick Heiress #2114
Strictly Temporary #2169

Silhouette Desire

The Magnate's Marriage Demand #1842
For Blackmail...or Pleasure #1860
Baby Bequest #1908
Bedded by Blackmail #1950
The Billionaire's Fake Engagement #1968
Bargaining for Baby #2015
Amnesiac Ex, Unforgettable Vows #2063

Other titles by this author available in ebook format

ROBYN GRADY

was first published with Harlequin Books in 2007. Her books have since featured regularly on bestseller lists and at award ceremonies, including a National Readers' Choice Award, a Booksellers' Best Award, Cataromance Reviewers' Choice Award and Australia's prestigious Romantic Book of the Year Award.

Robyn lives on Queensland's beautiful Sunshine Coast with her real-life hero husband and three daughters. When she can be dragged away from tapping out her next story, Robyn visits the theater, the beach and the mall (a lot!). To keep fit, she jogs (and shops) and dances with her youngest to Hannah Montana.

Robyn believes writing romance is the best job on the planet and she loves to hear from her readers. So drop by www.robyngrady.com and pass on your thoughts!

This story is dedicated to another gorgeous Zack.
Mission accomplished!

With much thanks to my wonderful editor, Shana Smith,
for her continuing belief and support,
as well as to Jessica Alvarez for her fabulous input.
Much appreciated, ladies!

One

Cool. Unruffled.

Nothing rattled Zack Harrison's cage.

He viewed Denver's unseasonal snowfall this afternoon as a picturesque bonus more than an inconvenience. Today's setback with regard to his latest acquisition strike was another challenge, not a reason to rant. Achieving a goal *should* involve effort, Zack decided as he shrugged into his overcoat, thanked the concierge and collected his briefcase. He'd simply need to get more…*inventive* was the word.

However, his patience was sorely tested when it came to the press. Last month's beat-up was nothing short of laughable. Apparently he was a fiend who left underprivileged families homeless in order to expand his evil empire. And what about that recent piece questioning his treatment of an ambitious actress he'd been seeing? Without exception he treated women with respect but, from the get-go, he and Ally had agreed upon "fun and casual," not "if I don't see a diamond ring, I'll expose your darkest secret." As if blackmail would work. Unlike his father and siblings, *this* Harrison didn't give a rat's behind what people thought.

But on this late-spring afternoon, as he strode from the hotel's entrance, yanked open the waiting cab's back passenger door and zipped inside the toasty cabin, Zack's calm fled and he jumped back in his seat. He took a moment to adjust and study his unexpected company before leaning forward to tap the driver's shoulder.

"Your last fare forgot something."

The cabbie angled around. "A wallet?"

"No," Zack said. "A baby."

The other back door swung open. A cool rush whooshed inside along with a woman wearing a hooded cherry-red coat. She set a matching overnighter on her lap and promptly slapped the door shut against the howling drifts. Blowing warmth into her cupped hands, her attention shifted. Beneath the red hood, curious eyes the color of new violets slid from the infant car seat carrier up to Zack and back again.

He considered her face, those eyes, and his chest grew unusually warm. He hadn't met this woman before and yet something in her glittering gaze had him wondering if he knew her. Perhaps he'd simply like to.

"I was in such a hurry, I didn't see you get in," she said, wrapping her manicured hands around the lip of her case. "Actually I couldn't see much at all. Crazy, isn't it? All this snow, I mean."

A slow smile hooked one side of his mouth as Zack's gaze drank her in. "Yeah," he said. "Crazy."

"It seems like the concierge called a cab ages ago. I walked to the curb to see if I could hail one down. I thought it might never come."

Zack's smile faded. He'd stolen her ride? When he'd checked out a few minutes ago, the front desk had organized a cab. Exiting the hotel's foyer, he'd merely assumed.

He leaned forward again, spoke to the driver. He'd pick off

this easier problem then take care of that other more complicated baby matter next.

"Are you answering a call?"

"Just back from dropping a fare at the airport." The man behind the wheel pushed a maroon beret back on his brow before flicking on the meter. "Thought I'd swing in here and try my luck. No one's going out in this weather 'less they have to."

"The airport." Red Riding Hood tipped forward, too. "That's where I'm headed. I need to get back to New York for an interview first thing tomorrow. I'm a features writer for *Story Magazine*." Her bright look said, *You've heard of it, right?*

Acting suitably informed and impressed despite his aversion, Zack nodded and said, "Of course," a moment before she dragged back the hood. The shadow framing her face lifted and Zack forgot to breathe.

Other than her cheeks, which were flushed a healthy pink, her complexion was as flawless as porcelain. Her hair, a luxurious mane, rested like a sable mantle over two slim straight shoulders. Her violet eyes were so vibrant their light penetrated and illuminated places he hadn't known existed.

He'd dated some beauties in his time, women who drew attention when they floated into a room and were comfortable exerting their power over the opposite sex. But Zack couldn't recall having met a female whose company literally left him short on air, and not only because of something as superficial as looks. In the clear depths of her eyes…the poised yet innocent manner with which she listened and spoke…

Quite simply, this woman glowed.

After today's unproductive meeting with the owner of this building he was ready to kick back and get home—home being the two-story private cabin he chilled at whenever he stopped in town. But the delectable Red was obviously in a hurry, eager to leave Denver and its freak weather behind. He'd be happy to play the gentleman and wait for another cab.

Which also meant she and the driver could work out between them what to do about this baby, who, thankfully, was still sound asleep.

Peaceful.

Zack looked harder.

Almost *too* peaceful. He had the damnedest urge to check each tiny finger curled over that wrap to make certain they were warm.

Red was peering at the baby, too. "I see you have a little one to worry about. She's gorgeous." She sighed then drew away. "I'll ask the concierge to call and see where my cab is."

As she turned to find her door's handle, Zack's muscles clenched and he caught her sleeve. Red couldn't leave. She had it all wrong.

When her gaze hooked back—unsure, concerned—he released her arm and coughed out a hoarse laugh at the same time he glanced at the baby.

"This isn't *mine*."

The cabbie grunted. "Sure as heck ain't mine."

The woman blinked two sets of generous lashes and her lips twitched as if she wanted to smile but didn't dare. "She looks a little young to travel alone."

She. Zack had to ask.

"How do you know it's a girl?" The carrier, blanket and bonnet were as white as the snow piling up on the sidewalk and road.

"Well, her face is so sweet." Expression melting, Red curved the back of her hand over the baby's bonneted crown and a tiny pair of lips pursed in and out as if she were dreaming about dinner. "Rosebud mouth," Red went on. "Cute and tiny. She's too pretty to be a boy."

The driver drummed his thumbs on the wheel. "Meter's running, folks."

"Of course." Gathering herself, Red pulled away. "I'll let you go."

For a second time that day, Zack's calm evaporated. But

now his mouth went completely dry, and sweat broke on the back of his neck. This afternoon was supposed to finish with a quiet brandy in front of a toasty fire, not tossing a hot potato like this around. He didn't even like babies.... Or, more correctly, *they* didn't like *him*.

"What are we supposed to do with her?" he asked.

"Not *we*, pal." The cabbie slotted the shift into gear.

His voice deep, Zack spoke to the man who clearly wasn't his "pal." "I told you, she isn't mine."

Red slanted her head and a stream of sable spilled over one shoulder. "What's she doing here then?"

"Beats me. Who'd you drop off last?" he asked the driver.

"An eighty-year-old man with a cane." The cabbie slid his beret back again. "He was flying out to see family in Jersey, and he wasn't carrying no bassinet."

The cabbie's expression said, *Don't know your game, son, but don't try to dump your problems on me.*

Zack growled. How many times did he have to say it? The baby wasn't his! At least it seemed that Red believed him.

Her face had lost all color as if every drop of blood had rushed to her feet. Her question came out a struggled whisper as though she shouldn't speak the words too loud for fear they might be true.

"Do you think someone abandoned her?"

"Guess the authorities will have to figure that out."

Zack didn't like the situation—not a bit. He knew less than zip about babies and had every intention of keeping it that way. Marriage and its inevitable complications were the furthest things from his mind. But, in this matter...

Ah, hell, what choice did he have? Red was in a legitimate hurry and—no getting around it—he had been the one to make the find. Either the guy behind the wheel could outact Tom Hanks or he sincerely had no clue. God only knew how a baby could end up alone in the backseat of a cab.

Zack's gaze roamed the small sleeping form, those rosebud

lips, that button nose, and his heart swelled and dropped. Some things you simply couldn't shrug off.

After flexing his fingers, he slid a firm grip around the un-harnessed car seat's handle.

"I'll bring her to the police station." His voice was hushed now. He didn't want to wake her and maybe have her cry. "They can call Child Services."

"But they could take *ages* to collect her."

"I only know a baby doesn't sleep forever and I don't carry spare diapers around in my breast pocket."

Red quietly searched around the foot of the blanket. "There's a bottle here," she said, "some formula and a few diapers, too."

"The officers at the local precinct will be most appreciative."

She lifted an eyebrow. "I'm sure they'll be eternally grateful."

Zack narrowed his eyes at her. What was she after? He was a businessman, for Pete's sake, not a babysitter—no matter how cute the kid.

The driver adjusted his rearview mirror. "Should I drop you two lovebirds off at a café so you can nut this out?"

"We're not lovebirds." Zack gripped the carrier's handle more tightly while Red held his gaze for an interminably long moment before surprising him yet again. Her slim nostrils flared, her delicate chin lifted a notch.

Then she reached out and her hand closed over his.

The sensation of her palm pressing, fingers brushing, sent his thoughts and pulse leaping. In an instant he became intensely aware of her scent, subtle and citrus, and the fact that her left hand bore no rings. The idea she might be unattached—available—hijacked and toyed with his mind.

When her fingers moved enough to scoop beneath his, her nails teased his palm and a jet of heat, like the initial burst of a flame, licked a hot path through his veins. Pleasant. Tempting. His runaway thoughts bubbled with all kinds of possibilities that had nothing to do with a baby, except, perhaps, the making of one.

"You go on," she said as her fingers wrapped around the carrier's handle and his reluctantly eased away. "I'll take her back inside with me. I can't stand to think of her waiting in a police station. Who knows what types might be lurking around."

Zack opened his mouth to argue. Red had a flight to catch. But in truth he couldn't disagree about the police station; not the best environment for an infant who'd need attention once she woke. And the instinct that rarely failed him said this woman was competent and trustworthy. The baby would be in good hands until the proper authorities stepped in. After that...

At the twinge beneath his ribs, Zack set his jaw and squared his shoulders.

After that, no doubt the mother would show up, all teary but relieved, and the family would have a good story to share at the kid's twenty-first.

But, for now, Red needed a hand to battle the snow and get them both inside.

He shifted. "I'll help you back in."

"No need."

Before he could insist, she'd opened her door. Standing with her overnight case in one hand, she waved in the direction of the hotel entrance with the other. Zack glanced out the back window. Through swirls of snow, a uniformed bellman was striding over, monster umbrella fending off the inclement weather.

James Dirkins, the current owner of this hotel, had refused his first offer on behalf of Harrison Hotels, but at this moment Zack was more determined than ever. When he snared the deal, bought this hotel, his first priority would be to cover that forecourt. Such a basic thing. No wonder occupancy was down.

After handing her luggage to the bellman, Red slid out the carrier. She had the good grace to flash a quick smile goodbye before the bellman shut the door and Zack watched them shrink then vanish into the white.

"So, you going to the airport, pal?"

Gaze still on the drifts, Zack murmured, "A private address."

"You want me to guess?"

But Zack wasn't listening.

Red...

He didn't even know her name.

"You could buy your own cab the way the meter's clicking over," the driver said. "Not that I'll complain."

Zack's ears pricked, his stomach jumped and he sat straighter. Was that the wind he heard gusting outside or a baby's cry?

Squeezing his eyes shut, he counted to three but, wouldn't you know, the urge only grew. Wasn't often Zack Harrison felt cornered. Beaten. But now he groaned, whipped out his wallet, dropped a bill over onto the front seat and told the driver, "Wait here. As long as it takes. I'll be back."

Trinity Matthews knew precisely what she'd gotten herself into.

Hours of waiting—and worrying—in a city where she knew no one; the naturopath she'd met and interviewed today for *Story* didn't count. And yet as she moved over the polished marble floor, heading for the hotel's sweeping timber reception desk with the baby carrier weighing on her arm, Trinity couldn't regret her decision.

Child Services did their best, but lines were long and resources low. At one time, she'd applied for a job in the department but personal experience with the system, as well as insight into herself, said she'd never cut it. So many neglected or abandoned children... She'd want to take home every one.

Glancing down, Trinity studied the sleeping baby and raw emotion gripped and thickened in her throat. Nobody asked to be tossed away. Nobody deserved to be, certainly not this little angel. If, in fact, abandonment were the case.

The echoing slap of footfalls on marble came from behind.

Trinity pivoted around. The man from the cab—the one with those incredible midnight eyes, that velvet smooth baritone and a smile that seemed strangely familiar—was jogging up toward her, dodging patrons and hotel staff, overcoat tails flapping behind. As he pulled up, a lock of dark hair fell over his brow and his broad shoulders rolled back as he drew in a deep breath. For a moment, Trinity felt a little out of breath herself. From head to foot, and everywhere in between, what an outstanding example of the male species. And there it was again… that niggle that whispered she knew him.

And maybe shouldn't trust him.

Then he introduced himself and the pieces of that puzzle all fell magically into place.

"I forgot to introduce myself," he said with a lopsided grin. "Zackery Harrison."

Trinity's eyes widened at the same time her stomach muscles clutched. Of course! Standing in the brighter light, who could dispute that dynamite build, the Hollywood looks, that authoritative air? In person, Mr. Harrison was indeed criminally sexy. From all she'd read, Trinity also knew he was a greedy, self-serving jerk.

But she wouldn't call him out on that here, now. This was neither the place nor time to give Mr. Harrison a piece of her mind. Siphoning in a settling breath, she schooled her features and introduced herself.

"I'm Trinity Matthews."

"Ms. Matthews," he said, looking as commanding as he did in his numerous celebrity shots, whether appearing barechested on his yacht or looking sophisticated and invincible in a tailored suit and tie. "I've given this situation more thought and I want to help."

Studying his charitable expression, she asked the obvious. "Why?"

Wariness flickered in his eyes before he smiled again. "Because I have some spare time and you need to get back to New York."

Trinity took in his intoxicating grin, white and inviting—the same smile that had reached out to intrigue her earlier in the cab. The same look that had seduced some of the country's most beautiful women and persuaded officials to trade people's homes for commercial profits. Her blood boiled to even think of self-serving, money-hungry corporate studs like Zack Harrison when so many people did without.

Which led back to the little person who needed her help now.

Whom did this baby belong to? What was her story? Trinity couldn't imagine anyone wanting to cast her aside. She was so perfect. So beautiful.

"I'll catch a later flight," she told Harrison. "I might not be a world expert where caring for new babies is concerned, but chances are I know more than you."

Weren't women supposed to be instinctive about maternal matters like feeding and soothing? Of course, Trinity knew better than most there were exceptions.

When Zackery Harrison crossed his arms, a subtle cue to have her capitulate and be on her way back to New York, Trinity set down the carrier and crossed her arms, too.

"I'm not leaving," she told him, "until I know she's okay."

"I have a place not far from here—"

"I said no."

Babies needed constant care and attention. *Love.* She wasn't certain Harrison even had a heart.

"My neighbors keep an eye on my place when I'm away," he pushed on. "Mrs. Dale is a spritely grandmother of ten. She doesn't like today's music or grasshoppers, particularly when her dianthuses are in bloom. But she adores babies. She used to be a foster mom."

Trinity suppressed a shudder. Despite her personal experience, certainly there must be a ton of fabulous ones. Still, she couldn't help her reflex reaction. For years the term "foster mom" had been interchangeable with *"monster mom,"* aka Nasty Nora Earnshaw, her own foster mother.

"Mrs. Dale ran her own home child-care business not so long ago," he went on. "Still has all the gear—high chairs, playpens. I know she'd be happy to help." His dark eyes glittered. "You don't want to miss your interview."

Trinity's fists unclenched.

Her job meant more to her than anything. It gave her the chance to travel and meet so many interesting and inspirational people. Individuals who touched others' lives in so many ways. After living in a small Ohio town most of her life, she loved working in New York. She'd made friends there. Had made herself a life.

Her profession was a fiercely competitive one. In these tough times, positions were hard to come by. With three coworkers laid off last week due to more budget cuts, she couldn't afford to rock the boat. But then there was this baby.

While patrons and hotel staff moved around them, going about their business, Trinity looked down again and her heart squeezed.

She didn't trust Zack Harrison. How much did he truly know about this neighbor of his, Mrs. Dale? Trinity's foster mother had given off a caring would-die-for-these-children impression, too. All a big fat lie.

"How can you be sure this miracle neighbor of yours will be in?" she asked.

"The Dales are homebodies. I've been in town a few days. When I passed by this morning, just before the snow began to fall, Mrs. D was hurrying inside her gate, back from taking one of her grandkids for a walk in the stroller."

Nibbling her lower lip, Trinity glanced around the busy foyer…at the helpful receptionist, the bellboy waiting patiently nearby, the concierge at his desk looking ready at a moment to rush over and help.

She made her decision.

"We're staying here. It's a good hotel. Great staff—"

"This baby's better off with someone who knows about children."

His voice held a warning note—low and deep—but he didn't look annoyed, merely determined. And, damn it, didn't he have a point? They'd already established they had no idea how long the authorities would take getting out. And if she put her own past experience and suspicions aside, Mrs. Dale could be precisely what this baby needed at this uncertain point in time. To be fair, how much of her reluctance was about what was best for the baby and how much about her own issues and personal dislike for Mr. Harrison?

Trinity gazed down at the baby, still sleeping soundly, and finally relented.

"Okay." She nodded. "We'll go."

"We?"

"I need to see her settled before…" Trinity shut down an image of the baby being taken away to God knows where, for however long, and ended by saying, "Before I leave."

Zack Harrison's features were angled in a strong, classical kind of way. His coal-fringed eyes reflected a character that was both comfortable with himself as well as with others, but they were also hypervigilant. Watchful while somehow resigned—the mark of a man who wielded power and was content in the knowledge that he was indeed a force.

Self-assured. Unapologetically so. But now Trinity saw another emotion shifting in his gaze.

Was it respect?

"In that case," he said, "we'd better go before our cabbie turns traitor and takes another fare."

At the same time he moved to claim the carrier's handle, so did she. When their hands met, skin against skin, heat on human heat, Trinity felt her face flush as her blood reacted and raced. With that lock of hair hanging over his brow, Zack looked across and grinned at her. Getting her rabid hormones under control, Trinity straightened.

"Before we go, I think it's only fair I admit that I know who you are."

His chin lifted. "I told you who I was."

"I read like everyone else, Mr. Harrison. You help run your family's hotel chain. You do whatever it takes to get whatever you want—" She hesitated but couldn't hold it back. "And you pride yourself on seducing beautiful women."

The grin froze on his face. "You subscribe to my fan club."

"Just so you understand—I'm agreeing to this only because I believe it's the best option for that baby."

"Not because I'm ruthless and irresistible?"

Her heart jumped and she fought the urge to lick suddenly dry lips.

"Definitely not because of that."

He seemed to loom closer, look hotter, as his eyes glittered, penetrating hers. "Well, now you have that out the way, we should go. Unless…"

Her antennae quivered. "Unless what?"

"We get this out of the way now."

"Get what out the way?"

"I thought you might want to kick my shin, slap my face. Pull my nose."

The tension locking her shoulders eased. She'd thought for a moment… Oh, but that was ridiculous.

"I'll try to restrain myself," she said.

He looked at her sideways as if he might be able to glimpse a well-hidden piece of her soul. "Ms. Matthews, you didn't think I was going to do something wholly in character, like take you in my arms and *kiss* you? Maybe even ravage you?"

Her cheeks caught light. The man was outrageous! "Of course not."

"I'm such a beast. How can you be sure?"

"I'm hardly your type," she pointed out. "Even if I were,

after these last few weeks of less than glowing publicity, you couldn't possibly want to draw attention to yet another incident." She slid a confident glance around the busy area. "We're out in the open. Everyone has cell phones and every cell phone has a camera."

Mr. Harrison's eyes lost their spark. His gaze turned dark, almost predatory.

"You think I care about gossip?"

"No. I don't." She cocked her head. "But maybe you should."

That devilish smile twitched and spread again.

"You're right. Maybe I should." He stepped unforgivably close while his gaze held her unforgettably still. "And maybe I should give the world something to really talk about."

Two

Zack slanted his head closer to Trinity Matthews's stunned violet-colored eyes and almost forgot that he'd been teasing. Making her pay.

She didn't know him from a lump of wood. What a laugh that she should make assumptions based on the tripe gossipmongers served up—and how typical. After all, she was one of them—a reporter for some rag-or-other he'd never heard of before today. Most publications shared a common code, turning a castaway line or suggestive photo into a sensation that had nothing to do with the truth and everything to do with building numbers and keeping their parasitic jobs.

Still, he was a good sport. He wouldn't hold any of that against Ms. Matthews, particularly when she was so darn cute all fired up, blushing and battling her conscience. Would she make a scene if he did the unimaginable and kissed her, or would she melt into his embrace and maybe make the front page herself?

Sorely tempted, his head dropped lower, but at the last moment, his trajectory veered and his attention fell again to the baby. He collected the carrier and headed for the hotel exit. A few seconds later, Trinity Matthews's heels were clicking double-time behind him.

Outside, from a gray Colorado sky buttressed by mountains, the snow was falling faster. When they were all safely back in the cab, Zack called Child Services on his cell while the meter ticked and Trinity watched the baby. Finally he spoke with a woman who asked for his number and address then said a representative would get back to him as soon as possible. She also said it was her obligation to inform the police of all details, including his. Perfect. Saved him.

As he ended the call, in hushed tones, Trinity asked, "What'd they say?"

"They'll get back to us."

"When?"

"When they can." *Soon,* he hoped. He slotted the cell away. "In the meantime, we'll pick up some spare diapers and head over to Mrs. Dale's."

When the authorities took away the baby, he'd pay for Trinity's return fare to the airport. With this good deed done and out of the way, he'd get to sipping that brandy before a toasty log fire. Zack was in half a mind to ask whether Trinity might like to join him, if only to see whether she'd leap at the chance to dress him down or betray her morality for curiosity and accept.

They stopped at a drugstore. The baby was still asleep when Zack returned to load the trunk with two bags of diapers, as well as wipes, additional formula, bottles and three small undershirts and one-piece outfits. As Zack well knew, in any venture, preparedness was the key. Besides, the pink suit had tiny ears on the hood like a cat or bear. Who could pass that up?

The baby was still pushing out pint-size *z*'s when half an hour later the cab swerved into his neighbors' long driveway.

Dusk had fallen over the peaceful, largely unpopulated district, which was bordered by giant firs, their branches burdened with the weight of new snow. A lonely streetlamp cast an eerie glow over the wintery ground but no light shone from the Dales' place. In fact, for the first time Zack could recall, that house appeared quite still.

Deserted.

Trinity was peering out the foggy window, too.

"No one's home." Studying the surrounding woods, she sat back and hugged herself. "We should have stayed at the hotel. Do you even get cell reception out this far?"

"If you're heading back in, you'd want to be quick about it." The driver upped the wiper speed and blades thrashed triple-time across the icy screen. "This is turning into a storm."

Fingers threaded on his lap, Zack thought for a moment then gave the driver instructions. "Continue on, a hundred yards down on your right."

"Hang on just a minute." Trinity clutched her seat belt like it was the only parachute on a plane going down. "Did you hear what he said? This snow's not letting up. If we're going back into town, we need to go now."

"The authorities have my details. They know where we're headed. We'll stay put until they get back to us."

In the growing shadows, her eyes flashed and those kissable lips tightened. She shook her head. "We're going back."

"Not an option."

"Why not?"

"You mean aside from being smart and staying out of this weather?"

He paused long enough to draw attention to wind gusting and whistling outside. When Mother Nature spoke, people did best to listen. Besides, he refused to set foot inside that hotel again until Dirkins had sufficient time to sweat over his offer. If he checked in tonight, the owner of that hotel would assume Zack had weakened and was prepared to sweeten the offer he'd made. That wasn't the case, no matter how much Zack sympathized with Dirkins's personal situation. A death in the family was never easy, particularly, he imagined, when it involved an only son.

The baby shifted. A tiny fist curled into the blanket. Zack held his breath while she yawned, stretched and squeaked at the same time a frown pinched her flawless brow.

He growled. *That did it.*

"My cabin's a minute's drive from here," he said. "Don't know about you, but I'd rather dance naked in that snow than be stuck in a cab when she wakes up crying."

The baby squeaked again, louder this time. Then her nose wrinkled before she settled fitfully again. Trinity pressed her lips together for a considering moment before her hold on the seat belt eased and reluctantly fell away.

"All right. We'll go to your place."

Wasting no time, Zack tapped the driver's shoulder and the cab pulled carefully out of the Dales' snow-clogged driveway. After the baby was put down again later, before the authorities arrived, he and Ms. Matthews could take time to reflect on the decisions they'd made, perhaps while sitting in front of a crackling fire with that brandy that felt so close now, he could almost taste it.

Despite her stand, animal instinct said she was as attracted to him as he was to her. Could be interesting getting to know her a little better.

Gazing out the window, Zack slowly smiled.

Who was he kidding? Truth was that he'd like to get to know Ms. Matthews, and her attitude, a whole lot more.

At the same time the cab rolled away from Zack Harrison's address, the full moon peeked out from beneath its heavy blanket of cloud. As a silvery glow illuminated the scene, Trinity could barely stop from gasping and rubbing to clear her eyes.

This was a *cabin?*

Zack, with the carrier and bags of baby supplies, was already striding through the drifts on his way to the covered entrance of the spectacular A-frame home. Flopping her coat's hood over her head, Trinity gripped her case and hurried after him. He pushed back the large timber door, flicked on a light and she stepped through into central-heated heaven. Marveling over her new surroundings, she blindly set her case on the hardwood floor.

The lower story was huge and open plan, various details of which hinted at exceptional wealth as well as a rustic homey welcome. To the right, the kitchen area was elevated one step and dressed in soaring polished oak with shining granite trimmings. At the far end of the room, a state-of-the-art media section was laid out before sumptuous connected leather recliners. In the center of a massive slate wall, a significant stone fireplace begged to be lit and have marshmallows toasted over gentle flames. A hallway off the foyer would lead to bedrooms, Trinity decided. As she drew back her hood, her gaze climbed a loft staircase that led to a mezzanine floor encased by carved timber rails.

Zack's husky words brushed her ear as he passed and explained, "The main bedroom."

She quivered. Main bedroom. *His* bedroom. A whirlpool of images swam up in her mind, the most vivid: Zack Harrison relaxing back against a strong, wooden headboard, rumpled sheet draped over lean hips, hard broad chest shamelessly on display, his expression self-assured…roguish and hot.

Hauling herself back, Trinity caught her breath. She wasn't here to fantasize about sleeping with a man who'd made sexual seduction his favorite personal pastime. Obviously she wasn't the only female he affected this way. The media spotted a new besotted squeeze on his arm every other month. But dwelling on his charisma—on that blatant sex appeal—had no place here, particularly when she'd made a fool of herself earlier at the hotel. She'd practically dissolved when she'd thought he might kiss her. Her skin flashed hot just thinking how he must have laughed when, eyelids growing heavy, she'd visibly trembled.

But he wouldn't catch her out again.

While Zack gently set down the carrier and supplies then maneuvered out of his overcoat, Trinity chased the butterflies from her stomach, slipped out of her coat as well then offered a neutral, totally honest statement.

"Your home is beautiful."

"I don't spend a lot of time here," he said, peeling back the carrier's light blanket, which had acted as a shield for the baby against the falling snow. "I hail from New York, like you. But you already know that."

She ignored his mischievous, pointed look and continued to study the room. "So this is a getaway?"

"My dad used to spend all his time at the office. To make it up to us, we'd always pack up and head off to Colorado for a break during snow season." He set his coat on the nearby rack, hung hers, too, then shucked out of his suit jacket before hooking that as well. "When I was older, I kept traveling out and found this area. We've got some amazing scenery. Nice people, too—the kind who are never too busy to nod and say hello when you pass on the street. I figured I might as well have a place on hand."

"But you don't have a vehicle in the garage?" Or there'd be no need for a cab.

"Engines like to be turned over regularly, so it's easier to rent something. When I flew in this time, there'd been a mix-up with the rental information. I don't exactly fit inside a bubble car." He gave his impressive shoulders an awkward roll to make his point then threw a glance toward the kitchen and collected the baby carrier again. "I'll put on some coffee. We can get her bottle set up while it brews."

Trinity knew she was stepping on dangerous ground but she couldn't keep her gaze off the impressive ledge of his shoulders in that white business shirt as she followed him into a large kitchen. The way his well-spaced shoulder blades moved in tandem with his purposeful, measured stride was enough to make her fingers itch to reach out and touch. In these more intimate surroundings—now they were alone—Zack's presence was a step away from spellbinding. Not that he'd need anyone to tell him that. *She* certainly didn't need to dwell on it a moment more.

And yet, as he set the carrier gently down again, wrung loose his tie and studied the baby—brow lined and dark eyes concerned—Trinity was more aware than ever of her physical reaction to his air of authority. His aura of masculine supremacy. That awareness made her flush from head to foot and everywhere in between. The reports were all true.

Zack Harrison must be the sexiest man alive.

"Should we sterilize something?"

Trinity dragged her focus away from the sweep of his full bottom lip then registered and answered his question.

"Yes. Absolutely. A bottle." Stepping forward, she crouched beside the carrier and examined the baby who, after earlier noises, appeared to have settled again. "I'll find the directions for the formula."

Carefully she slipped the bottle and formula canister out from where they rested at the foot of the carrier. Zack found a saucepan while she deciphered the formula's directions...although her attention wasn't entirely on the job.

Whistling a vaguely familiar tune while finding a coffeepot, Zack seemed at home here in this setting. And yet he spent most of his time in New York. Did he live in a Chelsea condo or a penthouse on Central Park West? Or was it the presidential suite of a family hotel? Hell, probably every Harrison came home to their very own multimillion-dollar penthouse.

"What's it like?" she asked, setting the formula down.

His back to her, Zack collected mugs from an overhead cabinet. "What's what like?"

"Owning all that real estate." *Pimping it out only to those who can afford the exorbitant rates.*

"I don't own Harrison Hotels exclusively." He pulled one end of his tie. With a zipping sound, the expensive strip of blue silk slid out and dropped in an abstract coil on the counter. "It's a family business."

"So you work every day with your parents and siblings?"

She'd always wanted sisters—or rather ones who would stay in her life rather than being moved on to another foster home after they'd become close. After a while, she'd given up wishing and hoping.

For a time, in between "then" and "now," she'd dreamed of having a family all her own, with a caring husband who would always stand by her, and at least one baby, but preferably two. She'd even picked out names. But over the years her plans had changed.

Zack was answering her question about siblings.

"We have our good days. We're like-minded in many respects." He found sugar then milk from a fridge that housed its own high-definition TV. "We're different in other ways, though. How about you? Do you have family?"

A familiar jab poked her ribs. It was one thing to sometimes think about what she'd once hoped for more than anything in the world. For anyone to ask her outright about whether or not she had any kind of family was quite another.

Trinity focused back on the formula. "Oh, nothing like that," she said in a remarkably even voice.

"Like what?"

"Like your family. Like…blood."

Not much of an answer but normally she didn't like to think about it let alone talk about her past. She definitely wasn't out to garner anyone's pity, particularly Zack-*I-have-it-all*-Harrison. Besides, the past was well behind her. What purpose would bringing it up here serve?

But then, peeling back the formula's lid, her gaze wandered again to the baby. Her throat closed over and for the first time in a long while she rethought that stand. From as far back as she could recall she'd been a private person. But wasn't this situation unique? No matter what she thought of his public image, Zack Harrison had given his time and opened up his house, not only to this baby but to her as well. Maybe this once she could share.

"Actually," she said, her heart beginning to pound, "I was a ward of the state."

She glanced over her shoulder. About to lift the coffeepot, Zack froze. His focus shifted to the carrier then skated over to her. His gaze penetrated hers so deeply she almost regretted opening her mouth. She wasn't a freak, just one of many ex-foster kids.

"That's why..." he began and she nodded.

"That's one of the reasons why I couldn't walk away."

He exhaled a long breath then poured steaming coffee that smelled both bitter and comforting. When both mugs were full, he met her gaze again. The surprise was gone from his eyes, but she wasn't much happier with the sympathy drawing on the corners of his mouth.

"Did you have a rough time?"

Her smile was thin. "Not everyone can land a Mrs. Dale."

"But you made good. All these years later working for—"

His brows knitting, he crossed over and handed her a mug while she contained a grin. She'd gleaned from his polite but vacant look earlier in the cab that he'd never heard of the publication.

"I work for *Story Magazine*."

"Ah, yes. *Story.*"

He took a long pull from his mug. She did the same, and almost sighed, the heat and flavor were so good. But while she concentrated on warming her palms, she felt his gaze tracing over the lines of her face.

"Ever interview a successful hotelier who rescues babies as a sideline?" he asked.

Meeting his midnight gaze, she cocked her head and pretended to be intrigued, which, in truth, she was. "Can't say I have."

"If you play your cards right, I could be available for questions later."

"I have a question for you now."

"I'm all ears."

She had the darnedest urge to say, *When you came so close in that hotel foyer earlier, was it because you really wanted to kiss me or because you wanted to put me in my place?*

Of course, she swallowed the urge, retacked her neutral smile and asked instead, "Can I have some sugar?"

He slowly smiled. "You can have anything you want."

He brought over the sugar bowl. She heaped in a good spoonful and took her time stirring. Leaning around her, he set the sugar bowl on the counter. His arm brushed hers as he tipped back but, although her stomach jumped, she gave no outward sign of how high her pulse had skipped. Rather, she dropped her focus to the baby again, taking in the healthy glow, the plump pink cheeks.

Attention on the baby now, too, Zack asked, "How old do you reckon she'd be?"

"Maybe three months. She looks well cared for."

"It doesn't make sense her being left alone like that. There has to be more to it."

An idea struck and a chill crawled up her spine. "Maybe she was abducted." It happened, and more than some people might think. Stories that made the news were only the tip of the iceberg. "Perhaps they'd planned a ransom and got cold feet at the last minute."

His voice was low and patient.

"Is that what happened to you?"

How she found herself in foster care? She shook her head but didn't feel a need to explain more. A man in Zack's situation, obviously so involved with his own family and position, couldn't possibly understand.

The baby gave a squeak. Then she squirmed and blinked open sleepy eyes. Both Zack and Trinity bent over the carrier while the baby yawned and tried to focus. Trinity's entire body flooded with a warmth she hadn't known existed—powerful yet soft and syrupy all at the same time.

"Her eyes are blue," she whispered.

"Do you think she's hungry?"

As if to answer, the baby let out a whimper, and another. When Zack hesitated, Trinity took control and folded back the blanket. By the time the harness was unclipped and the baby was out of the carrier, whimpers had grown to little sobs. Her heart tugging low in her chest, Trinity held the baby close. She was heavier than she expected but also easier to hold.

"Poor darling," she murmured against the velvet of that tiny cheek. "She must be wet. I'll take care of that. Can you handle the bottle?"

"Sure. No problem." He cast a tentative look at the canister. "You, uh, said there were directions?"

"On the side. Or do you want dibs on first diaper duty?"

He took a long step back. "I'll have the bottle ready when you come out."

She was shown to a downstairs bedroom with an attached bath. After she laid the baby on the bed and Zack set down a plastic bag of supplies, Trinity left to find a towel from the bath. Changing diapers could be a messy business; she didn't want to leave the bedspread soiled. Returning, she noticed a silhouette lurking in the shadows of the bedroom doorway. Zack.

"I wanted to make sure the baby didn't roll off the bed," he said.

"At three months or younger, she's too young to roll."

Even if she were four months, she wouldn't be able to roll more than once, and from her tummy to her back, not the other way around. She'd learned that when Nora Earnshaw had cared for an infant for a short time. A seven-year-old Trinity had spent all her spare time with that child. When the baby was taken away suddenly one day, she'd been so heartbroken and lonely; she'd barely eaten for weeks. The only saving grace was that the baby's new foster home had to be better than Nora's house. Maybe he'd even been adopted by a couple who never let him cry.

Zack smoothed a hand through his coal-black hair. "Then I guess I'll get that bottle underway."

Smiling to herself, Trinity watched him disappear then bent over to touch the sniffling baby's forehead with her own. To think a big, bossy man like Zack Harrison standing all the way back there. Anyone would think he was afraid of holding this little cherub, of bringing her close, whereas any person in their right mind would find it hard to let her go.

Ten minutes later, Trinity emerged from the bedroom feeling most pleased with herself. The baby wore a fresh diaper as well as an intent, curious expression in her gorgeous robin's-egg-blue eyes as if she wanted to thank this strange woman but didn't know how. In the kitchen, his cuffs folded back, Zack was busy shaking a full bottle over his wrist. The image was so incredibly sexy, as well as rather funny and tender, something unfamiliar shifted inside and Trinity cradled the baby all the closer. Did all men look slightly awkward yet undeniably hot when performing this kind of domestic feat? Zack was so focused on his task he hadn't noticed the liquid spraying on his previously immaculate hardwood floor. Talk about single-minded.

"Milk stains, you know," she said, crossing over.

His dark eyes flashed as he glanced up then down at the formula sprayed on the floor and his shoes. Grunting, he dropped a nearby dishcloth. Keeping a firm hold on the bottle, he rubbed the cloth over the damp area with a foot.

"The temperature needed checking."

"If you'd kept going," she teased, "there wouldn't be anything left in the bottle."

With a lopsided smile that did bone-melting things to her pulse, he held the bottle high.

"I'm happy to report the beverage is well mixed and—if I do say so myself—perfectly warmed."

"In that case…" She made to hand over the baby. "Would you care to do the honors?"

His smug smile vanished. "I'll take the next shift."

"She won't bite."

"How do you know?"

Trinity wondered what he'd do if she plunked the baby in his arms and told him to handle it. If she'd let him tell her what to do, she'd have been on her way back to New York and he'd be here all alone with an infant to care for. Lucky for him she wasn't a pushover.

Trinity headed for the open plan area. "I'll need a seat."

As he overtook her, a hot palm grazed the small of her back and that unfamiliar feeling filled her middle again, spreading heat up toward her chest and throat. For a mindless moment, she held on to the feeling before dragging herself back. Given Zack's lack of confidence in this area, it was up to her to stay on top of things.

Wouldn't this make a great story. Hotelier Magnate Admits To Failings.

Stopping at the dining table, Zack held out a carved wooden chair and, with a flourish, indicated she should sit. Trinity studied the chair's upright back and wrinkled her nose.

"Maybe something a little more comfortable."

Frowning, he pushed the chair back in. Next she was shown to one of those sumptuous white leather recliners. Feeling as if she were descending into a cloud, she seated herself. A lever on the recliner's side was lifted, a footrest whirred out and her legs rose until they were near horizontal. Zack couldn't have looked prouder if he'd single-handedly closed down a community hall to build yet another skyscraper—which he had just last month.

Finding the baby, accompanying Zack Harrison into the

middle of nowhere—this entire evening had been surreal. But reclining here with Zack looming closer left her feeling more than a little edgy. And curious. The media was awash with shots of his recent breakup with starlet Ally Monroe. So who was Zack seeing at the moment? Did he feel any guilt over business decisions that had hurt ordinary Americans? Was he as good in bed as the world envisioned him to be?

After meeting him, she'd wager he was even better. Any woman with half her quota of hormones would sizzle in his presence. Girls had probably mooned over him since middle school.

Zack was standing, legs braced, hands low on his hips. "What else do you need?"

She brought her focus back to the baby, who was peering up, a tiny frown pinching her brow while four little fingers wiggled above the turn of her wrap. "Can I have a hand towel? Something to mop up any excess?"

He handed over the bottle and she watched him stride away, drinking in the way his long, solid legs worked to create such a smooth, fluid gait. A moment later, he handed over a towel and, standing back again, squared those impressive shoulders.

"Good luck," he said in a mock-solemn tone that pried a smile from her lips.

"I'll report back on casualties," she replied, checking the measurements embossed on the bottle's side before lowering the nipple.

Alert baby blues opened wider. In a heartbeat, the baby had latched on and was sucking like she hadn't eaten in days. Trinity's stomach knotted tight. How long *had* it been since her last feeding? Where was her mother? Child Services knew of the situation, but how long before this little sweetheart was taken away?

Of course, the mother might be off searching for her right now. If that were the case, Trinity hated to think of the agony that woman must be going through. Much like her own mother before—

"No one's called back yet," Zack said.

Trinity's train of thought shifted back to the present. Zack was lifting a dining chair and setting it down beside her. Elbows on knees, he leaned forward and threaded his fingers. Trinity wondered why he didn't take a seat on a recliner. Maybe he was more comfortable keeping that bit of distance.

"I wonder when the police will arrive," she said, balancing the bottle in the *V* of her hand as the baby chugged.

"This weather's probably holding them up. I'll flick on the news channel soon to see if anything's been reported. Maybe give them a call myself to make sure all the right info was passed on." His gaze on the baby now, his chin tipped up and a shadow of a smile touched his lips. "You look like you're an old hand at this."

"She's the one doing all the work." And working at full steam!

Outside, the wind howled and, beyond a set of floor-to-ceiling French doors and windows, Trinity watched more snow fall while the baby settled down.

After a time, Zack shifted uneasily. "Shouldn't she be burped sometime soon?"

"Bet you'll look like an old hand at it."

He sat slowly back. "On second thought, you're doing a great job."

"For a big, tough corporate type, you really are a chicken."

"Sticks and stones."

But, while Zack might be hesitant to be hands-on, he did have a point about stopping to let the baby bring up wind. Trinity drew the near empty bottle from her mouth and, bracing herself, waited for the grumble. When the baby only released a quivering sigh and blinked slumberous, contented eyes, Trinity smiled.

Too easy.

She rested the baby against the left side of her chest while Zack moved to position the towel over her shoulder. Then she sat forward to pat and rub the baby's warm little back. Trinity's eyes drifted shut as her heart swelled.

Dear heaven, she felt so small. So precious.

Minutes passed and, still patting, Trinity became curious. Then a little worried. Nothing was happening. Perhaps she ought to feed her the rest of the bottle. Maybe Zack should make another one, too. Or wasn't she burping her right?

Zack must have read the uncertainty in her eyes. He sent over an encouraging look.

"Give her a chance. Her digestive system's only new."

She gave him a look. *How do you know so much?*

He shrugged. "Lots of nieces and nephews."

Two minutes later, he was sitting on the edge of his chair, clasped hands resting against his chin, his brow lined. "Maybe pat a little harder."

Trinity's back went up. She didn't need the added pressure. "Maybe you could go and organize your next big takeover."

"I'm taking a couple of days off."

"Then maybe go make us something to eat." Instead of sitting there, watching her every move and making her all jittery.

He stayed put. "How do you know I can cook?"

"Same way you knew I could change a baby."

He chuckled, then, looking suitably magnificent, he got to his socked feet. "In that case, prepare to be dazzled."

She rolled her eyes and kept patting. "Let me guess. Macaroni and cheese."

"You do realize that you are now in the wild. I'm all that separates you from any kind of sustenance and starvation."

The baby answered for her, with a loud, most unladylike burp.

His jaw dropping, Zack drew a set of fingers through his hair. "Seems her digestive system is working just fine."

Encouraged, Trinity eased out of the recliner onto her feet

then patted some more. The baby rewarded them with another belch. Bringing the baby away from her shoulder to examine her face, Trinity beamed.

"Oh, she looks completely satisfied."

That's when the baby burped again. But this time, wind wasn't the only thing she brought up.

Three

With that third big burp, not a whole lot stayed down.

The first priority—*bathe the wailing baby!*—was performed with much haste in the nearby laundry sink. Trinity found the task a slippery business, but when the baby had finally settled down from her upset, the kicking, splashing and happy squeals had made it a surprisingly enjoyable job as well.

After the baby was dried, powdered, rediapered then dressed in one of the outfits bought earlier in town, Trinity swapped her own soiled blouse for a clean one. Hours of rocking, singing and cooing, interspersed with more *measured* bottle feeds, followed. Far from laying bricks or digging holes, but energy requirements were surprisingly high. Trinity supposed she could have laid the baby back in her carrier and hoped for the best—that she wouldn't whine—but those big blue eyes were so trusting, she simply couldn't.

Zack busied himself preparing dinner for the adults—steak and salad—of which not a single bite touched their lips. She was too occupied with the baby, and Trinity supposed Zack might feel guilty eating when she couldn't. He also made a cot of sorts in one of the recliners—comfortable, high enclosures, plenty of room. When the baby eventually shuddered out one last exhausted sigh and snuggled in, hopefully for the night, Trinity lowered her gently down into her bed and gazed at the peaceful sight for a long, thankful moment. Then she took her weary self and heavy arms off for a lovely hot shower.

Her choice of clothing afterward fell between a business suit or red silk pajamas…large jacket, long pants, all lined with soft brushed cotton. Matching slippers. Easy decision. In the privacy of the bedroom, she slipped into the soft silky folds, feeling too exhausted to worry about whether her attire was appropriate in the company of a man she knew only by reputation, and a bad reputation at that. But she doubted Zack would have the energy to goad. If he was half as tired as she was, he wouldn't notice whether she stumbled out wrapped in a black cape and gnashing a set of fangs.

Damp hair caught in a messy bun, feeling squeaky-clean and ready to collapse, Trinity lumbered into the living room. She stopped at the foot of the stairs.

But for the rush of wind outside, the house was eerily quiet. The room was completely dark, too, except for the flickering glow emanating from the far wall. Hugging herself, Trinity edged closer. Over the top of the recliners, a glorious sight bit by bit came into view.

Crouched beside the fireplace, her handsome host was busy tending crackling orange-and-blue flames…a hypnotic sight that had Trinity's lips parting to take in a dash more air. With slow, shifting shadows moving over his body—and the chiseled planes of his face—he seemed to sense her presence and glanced over. His gaze intensified then wandered to absorb her every inch, from the top of her wild bun all the way down to the red pom-poms on her feet. His study was so deliberate—so unapologetically favorable—it was more a self-indulgent, scorching touch. In the space of those few seconds, she'd never felt more like a woman. More desirable.

With just a look.

In one fluid movement, he pushed to his feet and set the poker blindly against the fireplace then moved nearer.

"You look ready for bed."

His words—low, husky—enveloped her as he stopped an arm's length away. A heartbeat later, when his scent wove into her lungs, Trinity involuntarily quivered inside and out. The seductive nature of the shadows, the blatant power of his presence... She felt so out of time and place, so unlike herself—if Zack touched her now, God help her, she might forget everything of which she disapproved and simply melt into a puddle at his feet.

"You were incredible." His lidded gaze dipped to her lips and his chest rumbled. "You must be exhausted."

Her mouth suddenly gone dry, Trinity tried to clear her swimming head. Yes, she was exhausted. Clearly more exhausted than she'd even thought.

"I knew she'd go down eventually," she said.

"At one stage I had my doubts." He flicked a look over at the baby sound asleep in her makeshift bed. "I can't see her waking anytime soon."

"Let's hope. I don't have one more verse of 'Bye Baby Bunting' left in me."

He tipped his head toward the fireplace.

Her eyes had adjusted more to the lack of light. A thick quilt was lain out with plump white pillows propped up against the other recliners.

"I've imagined enjoying a brandy before a quiet fire since four o'clock this afternoon. Care to join me?"

Trinity's pulse rate picked up a notch. After having spent the previous hands-on hours with him helping where he could, she might feel a little less hostile toward him, but not nearly enough to agree to lying in front of a flickering fireplace, sipping a glass of forty proof. But before she could decline, Zack threw up his hands.

"Yes, I know you think I'm a wolf—"

"Along with anyone else who picks up a magazine or goes on the web."

He exhaled but his mouth managed to retain his sexy smile. "*Anyway,* I give my word I won't use my apparently world-renowned seduction techniques to take advantage of the situation."

"And I should believe you why?"

"Because you're not my type, remember?"

Trinity paused. She had said that back at the hotel and anyone who understood the meaning of the saying "water meets its own level" knew it was true. That didn't negate the fact that Zack Harrison was hot and irresistible and a natural born flirt. Far better to play it safe.

"Maybe I should make myself a cup of cocoa."

But when she made a move toward the kitchen, he headed her off. "Let's be civilized about this and meet halfway. Not brandy or cocoa. I propose red wine."

"You really don't like to be beaten, do you?"

Rubbing a hand over the broad expanse of his white T-shirted chest, he groaned. "Come on, Trin. Cut me a break. It's late. We're both beat. Let's share a drink and chill a little before we crash."

She held that breath. Was this poor puppy-dog act one of many from his repertoire—or was she overestimating her own appeal? He dated models, movie stars and heiresses, not girls on strict budgets who lived in studio apartments in Brooklyn. Hell, maybe deep down she *wanted* him to flirt with her. Maybe even kiss her. She wondered what her friends—her boss—would say. They all knew how she'd felt about men of his ilk. How she *still* felt.

But he was right. It was late. They were tired. She could let her guard down a little.

"Brandy might knock me out completely," she smiled and admitted, "but a glass of red wine would be nice."

In the firelight, his dark eyes glittered with a grin before he crossed to a cabinet that housed a small bar.

Her gaze took him in from top to barefoot toe. In that white T-shirt and black sweatpants he'd changed into earlier, he cut the figure of a prime athlete. The T-shirt's fabric fell over the contours of his broad shoulders in an easy, tantalizing way that left her wondering who could ever weary of the sight. His legs were long and, from the firm sway of his body as he found bottles and glasses, obviously strong. As Trinity made herself comfortable on the quilt against the downy pillows, she was aware of every fiber relaxing and, at the same time, switching on to an unprecedented buzzing high. Probably not smart but, right now, it felt heavenly.

He brought over a glass for her, a snifter for himself and settled down a respectable distance to her left. After inhaling the wine's bouquet, she sipped and smiled as the smooth warmth slid down her throat.

"Good?" he asked.

"Hmm, very."

Satisfied, he leaned back against his pillow, tasted again, then hissed back through his teeth, clearly enjoying the burn of his brandy. But then his brow pinched and he glanced from the fire back at her.

"You know, we really ought to eat something," he said.

She settled farther into the pillows. "Let's sit here and just do nothing for five minutes."

"So I won't suggest you text your boss. You know you won't make it back to New York for breakfast."

Trinity's insides pitched at the thought of having to explain why she needed a day off when there must be a pack of people who would die for a chance at her job. But then she let her eyes close and she sighed, too exhausted to think about that now.

She murmured, "Five minutes."

Sometime later, Trinity felt something drift over her waist. Jerked back from sleep, she gasped and her eyes snapped open, but then she released that breath. Beyond the soft crackle of the fire and its shifting shadows, she recognized a man—Zack— settling a spare quilt over her legs.

"If the baby wakes during the night," he said, collecting his snifter again, "I'll get her."

Reclining again, Trinity's lips twitched. How did he intend to manage a messy diaper change? But the thought was a sweet one. And out of character, she thought. In his everyday life, she imagined Zack Harrison delegating all the mundane stuff, from RSVPing to five-star events to picking up the dry cleaning or sending a prospective female companion a stunning display of long-stemmed roses.

Bet his florist expenses are outrageous.

Overhead, something crashed and clattered on the roof. A branch whipped by the wind against the tiles? Trinity huddled down farther and inched the quilt higher. This snowstorm was really pulling up its sleeves. Could it possibly get any worse?

As the wind howled on like an angry beast outside, together they watched the fire's gentle flames lick and curl and spit. The atmosphere was lulling…hypnotic. After a time, Zack spoke.

"You're falling asleep."

Trinity roused herself. "I was just losing myself in the pictures."

"Pictures?"

"In the fire."

He swirled his brandy. "You're an artistic type."

"Right-brained, I guess you'd say." Thinking of the striking image Zack Harrison had drawn earlier—what an amazing natural form model he'd make—she indulged in a secret smile. "I like to sketch."

"I never made it past stick figures. How are you at physics, chemistry?"

Covering her mouth, she feigned a yawn.

"All right." His teasing gaze challenged hers. "So tell me. What do you see in the fire?"

"Sometimes I see animals," she said. "Sometimes people's faces."

"And tonight?"

Thoughtful, she angled her head and lost herself in the snaking hypnotic heat of those flames. "I see a baby. I see bottles and giggles, and a few tears. I'll probably dream about all that, too."

"You don't sound as though you'd mind."

Her gaze dropped. Was it that obvious? Her shoulder came up as she confessed, "She's a real cutie. It's going to be hard saying goodbye."

Out the corner of her eye, she saw his brandy swirl again and caught a whiff of its distinct bouquet before he pointed out, "Imagine how happy her parents will be."

"Yes." She tried to push aside her doubts—her own experience as a displaced child never reclaimed—and pinned on a smile. "I'll imagine that."

Zack maintained his own neutral look. His jaw didn't flex. Nostrils didn't flare. And yet he couldn't have been more affected.

From the start, Trinity Matthews had done curious things to his normally lucid state of mind, even with claws out, having a go at him. Sitting here while they talked and joked in the firelight had only served to make him hyperaware of that point.

Despite the fact that she disapproved of his personal life—based on trashy tabloid news, he might add—he was sorely attracted to her. He wanted to reach over, bring her close. Damn it, he wanted to *kiss* her. And in a slow, all consuming, let's-not-get-out-of-bed-for-a-week kind of way.

The simmering awareness in Trinity's liquid eyes, the engaging vibe she gave off when she let her guard down… If he traced a fingertip around the curve of her cheek, dropped his head over hers, would she slant toward him? Would she object if he scooped her up and dragged her off to his bed? The temptation was real—ridiculously so.

And that set him back.

Not because he was uncomfortable with any aspect of physical attraction, particularly when the person he wanted was so intelligent, competent and full of her own brand of fire. He admired anyone who wanted to stand by a strong opinion—even when they were wrong. His concern stemmed more from the peculiar sense of depth of his attraction to Trinity Matthews. He'd been intrigued by women before but not this way. Frankly the awareness he was experiencing at this precise moment was a little unsettling.

Clearly it was a product of these unusual circumstances. Here they were—isolated, sharing an unanticipated, highly emotive experience. Yes. That must be the reason for it. This unshakable, unrelenting need.

For several moments, he swirled his drink and stared into the fire. When he'd composed himself—physically, mentally—he pushed to his feet then ran a hand through his hair.

"Guess I'll grab a shower."

Looking delicious in those oversize pj's, lounging against those pillows, Trinity summoned a sleepy smile. "I'll hold the fort."

Before he surrendered to the beast within, still scratching and begging to be freed, Zack grabbed his cell off the kitchen counter, climbed the stairs and strode into his loft bedroom. Truth was, if it weren't for the baby, he'd probably open that cage and see what treats might be forthcoming. But after hearing that poor kid cry after her postbottle accident, watching how well Trinity had cared for her, the least he could do was slap a lock on that door—for the time being at least. All the world knew he wasn't a family-of-his-own type, however, here and now that child must be their number one priority. But once she was settled elsewhere, whether that be back with her mother or in the hands of the state—

Flinching, he ripped off his T-shirt.

The end result was out of his hands.

Two minutes later, hot water was spraying his back while, with one palm pressed against the glass, Zack took time to lather up his front. When his cell phone rang, his first thought was: *go away. Call back.* But then his brain clicked into gear and, soapy and dripping wet, he reached out to snatch up the phone. The voice belonged to the woman from Child Services he'd spoken with earlier, a Cressida Cassidy.

"I'm sorry I didn't get back to you sooner," Ms. Cassidy said. "I wanted to assure you that the authorities have been informed and a representative from both that department and my own will call tomorrow. The weather's abysmal. Impassable. I hope you don't mind caring for the baby overnight."

"No." The bathmat already sopping beneath his feet, Zack wiped water off his face. "I mean, that's fine."

"Has she settled down?"

"Without a moment's trouble."

Ms. Cassidy didn't need to know about the baby's red face when she'd hurled, or how he'd considered bundling her up and rushing her to the nearest clinic despite the weather when she wouldn't settle down before getting into the laundry tub half-full with tepid water. Being a parent was said to be the most difficult job in the world. After tonight he believed it.

Only proved again—he was *so* not ready. He didn't mind doing his bit, but nothing and no one—including family—could convince him he was ready for this kind of deal. Marriage. Kids. He liked his life just the way it was.

"Mr. Harrison, there is one more thing I need to say."

Grabbing a towel from the rack, Zack listened up. After a few seconds, he checked the display screen and frowned. Damn it. Lost signal.

Another branch crashed onto the roof and his gut jumped before he made a beeline to the bedroom phone. That line still worked. Ms. Cassidy would call again—she had his landline number—and a time would be set for collection to take place.

Not that *collection,* as a word, sat too well.

While the wind howled through a thousand treetops outside, he crossed to a chest of drawers. He needed something suitable to wear. Rifling through socks, he grinned, but he didn't own a pair of red silk pajamas. If he wasn't thinking straight, Trinity wouldn't be wearing red silk, either. She wouldn't be wearing anything at all.

At the same time a particularly angry gust shook the rafters, his towel slipped to the floor. Scanning the ceiling, Zack held his breath, waiting for the inevitable crash of a loose branch or two to land on the roof. The crash came—an almighty clattering *thump*—then the lights flickered, once, twice, and the roller-coaster evening took another unexpected turn.

Downstairs, the fridge clunked over and off. The single light emanating from the bar snuffed out. But for the flickering fire glow, the room would have been left in an impenetrable shroud of darkness.

Trinity remembered to breathe.

Obviously the storm had caused problems with the electricity. Maybe the blackout would last a few hours, maybe only a few minutes. The saving grace was that the baby was sound asleep and the kitchen was equipped with gas burners should milk need to be warmed.

Still, Trinity held her bottom lip between her teeth as she shuffled deeper under the top cover and brought the downy warmth up around her chin. With wide eyes, she scanned a room filled with suddenly spooky-looking shadows. Truth was she didn't much like the dark, not from as far back as she could recall, and there were at least a dozen reasons why.

Hurried footfalls sounded on the stairs, a padding that sent an eerie echo through the room. She pricked her ears, angled around and barely made out a figure, which came to a stop near the door. Something clicked and rattled then the figure moved again and—

Vanished?

Trinity's heartbeat began to pound in her chest, in her ears.

A moment later, something brushed her arm. Her head whipped to that side at the same time she leaped near out of her skin. While she strangled the covers close to her throat, in the light of the fire she caught the face and blew out a long, shaky breath. Of course, there was no need for her pulse to be sprinting a hundred-yard dash. Who on earth else would it be?

Zack's deep voice rumbled out from the dancing shadows. "You okay?"

She pasted on a blasé face. "I'm fine."

"You look a little shaken."

"Jeez, I don't know why. Sitting here with the lights out and the mother of all storms lashing around outside. It was the ideal time for you to sneak up on me like that."

"Can I help calm you down, hold your hand?"

Even though he was teasing, the need to recoil was outweighed by the urge to lean forward and say, *Yes, please.* Tamping down that impulse, she lifted her chin and calmly collected her glass.

"I don't need anyone to hold my hand."

Her gaze curved around the strong angle of his jaw, down the thick column of his throat and lower. Then she frowned, squinted. When she realized, her brain began to tingle. She swallowed deeply but her voice still came out a croak.

"What are you wearing?"

He glanced down as if he'd only now remembered, then stated the obvious. "A towel."

She tried to give a casual nod, like it was no big deal that this dark-haired Adonis was crouching beside her, bare-chested, practically naked. The slightest shift of those massive thighs and, with the firelight's help, nothing would be left to the imagination. Not that he seemed the least perturbed by his state of dress…make that *undress*. Hell, he might have paraded that body every other day to women he barely knew. And those arms…

Her eye line ran over that nearest bulging bicep and she swallowed again.

Clearly his body had been crafted from polished bronze. And he smelled so *fresh,* a combination of evergreen and musk. Her fingers itched to stroke up the toned ridges of his abdomen. Her palms ached to grip and rub those amazing pecs.

Then he was standing and that towel looked as if it was hanging on to those lean hips by nothing more than a prayer.

"…want some?" he asked.

Her attention leaped up from his chest to his face and, more precisely, the grin glinting in those dark eyes. Her jaw felt as slack as soft toffee. She'd been so engrossed, now she couldn't summon the good sense to answer whatever question it was that he'd asked and she wouldn't mind betting Zack knew it.

She couldn't pretend that she'd heard all his question. "Want some—" Her throat convulsed again. "Some what?"

His grin slanted more. "Wine."

She set her glass aside. "I'd better not indulge anymore."

His six-pack clenched as he chuckled. "Occasional indulgence, Trinity, is a must."

"I prefer sticking to the straight and narrow."

"Straight and narrow, huh?" He held her gaze with his for a long, unsettling moment then grunted and headed for the bar. He poured a second brandy as he asked, "So, was it bad?"

"Was what bad?"

"The breakup." He sent a knowing look over one bare shoulder. "I'm guessing it was and that it was recent."

Her neck and face began to glow with a blush he would never see, thank God. "What on earth would make you ask something like that out of the blue?" And, despite her affront, she had to know. "What makes you think I had a breakup?"

"Your attitude. My experience."

"With women?"

"That's right."

"Well, sorry to disappoint you, Dr. Phil, but I don't have time to date."

"Now that *is* a problem."

"What that is, Mr. Harrison, is none of your business."

He sauntered back, the towel slipping more with each step. He sipped and evaluated her again until that blush had devoured her entire body and she sat up straighter, defiant.

"Is that another one of your tactics? Standing over people, trying to make them feel small while you make yourself feel big."

She imagined a significant portion just below the knot in his towel jumped as if to answer her at the same time he exhaled. "So it *was* bad."

Reflex said to laugh, tell him to take his brandy and questions someplace else. But this was his house. And, damn it, he was right. *Bad* pretty much summed up the end of her last relationship. She slumped into the pillows.

"He was kind and considerate and a terrific listener. He also didn't like kids."

His head went back. "You'd gotten that far?"

"He hadn't proposed, if that's what you mean. But I think it says a lot about a person if the mere mention of children makes them shudder."

"At the risk of defending the guilty, men can have a slow uptake on that particular subject."

"And why is that?" She really wanted to know.

"Because if we go all gooey at the mention of children, some women might see that as a sign we want to…want to—"

"To commit?"

"Yeah. That." He nodded at the covers. "Mind if I join you? Of course, I'll get rid of the towel first."

Her breath caught but he was only teasing again. "Translation being you'll change into something more appropriate."

He headed out. "That, too."

A moment later, rattling came from the kitchen then a stream of light clicked on—a flashlight. Its arc waved once over the room before fading into another area.

Relaxing, Trinity snuggled into her makeshift bed, eternally grateful for the fire's light as well as its warmth. With the electricity down, the radiator would be out, too, unless it was powered by gas like the stove. Of course, there was always a possibility of sharing body heat.

As a pulse deep inside her kicked off, she scolded herself and snuggled down more.

Don't even consider it.

When Zack returned, he wore drawstring pants and a loose fitting T-shirt, most likely found in the laundry room. She'd seen a basket of clean clothes sitting on the counter when she'd bathed the baby earlier.

"I checked around outside," he said. "Snow's pretty deep."

"And still falling?"

"It's let up some, but this is not a night to be out. Hopefully by tomorrow sometime, the skies will be clear and the electricity will be back on. In the meantime, the stove, radiator and water are powered by gas, so we shouldn't freeze, and the baby's bottles and warm baths are covered." He looked into the fire. "The woman from Child Services called just before the lights went out."

Zack explained that Ms. Cassidy had assured him she would be out to take care of the baby issue as soon as possible. Trinity told herself she ought to be relieved. She could get on with her life. Get back to New York. But she couldn't help wondering about that baby's future, immediate as well as long-term. Where were her parents?

Lowering beside her, Zack grabbed a spare quilt and spread it over his legs and around his ribs at the same time he visibly shivered.

"It's freakin' freezing out there," he said. "And black. I can't remember the last time the lights went out."

"It's annoying," she admitted.

The child inside her whispered, *And just a little scary.*

He seemed to read her mind. "Could be the perfect time to share some ghost stories."

The look she sent was pained. "I don't think so."

"I remember when I was perhaps ten," he went on, as if he hadn't heard, "Dad took his usual few days off from being stuck behind his desk and the family came out here to Denver, but our regular chalet was double booked. The only place available was a run-down building that had once been a barn." His voice lowered. "Or so the story goes."

"I don't believe in ghosts, if that's where you're headed."

"Neither did I. Until that night."

Huffing, she pulled the covers higher. "You are so not the type to believe in things that go bump in the night."

"Are you?"

"Not the supernatural kind."

She caught his curious look and, knowing she'd said too much, she diverted the conversation. Might as well hear his story.

"So, you were all staying in an old barn."

"That had been renovated decades before to include a kitchen, living room, bedrooms in the loft. The electricity didn't go off like here tonight," he said, picking up the thread. "But only a handful of lightbulbs worked. The fireplace was covered in cobwebs. The walls and roof creaked enough to have my sister biting her nails. I think that's where it began."

"Your belief in the other side?"

"No. Sienna's gnawing at her fingers. Still does it to this day." Leaning back, he latched his own fingers behind his head and those delectable biceps bulged. "Anyway, the light in the boys' bedroom blew."

"How many brothers do you have?"

"Three. Mason, Dylan and Thomas." He pulled a mock-serious face. "We weren't scared, you understand."

She suppressed a grin. "Oh, I understand."

"But the wind was blowing like tonight, and when that light-bulb exploded, we all happened to need a glass of water at the same time. Thomas, the youngest, shot out the room first. The rest of us followed on his heels. Our parents were sitting in the musty living room on couches that needed condemning decades before. My father was fuming, vowing to sue whoever botched our reservation, which he later did. He said if a good enough gust came along, the whole place would fly away."

"Where was your sister?"

"Sienna was already snuggled up on my mother's lap. She's the baby. Always will be."

Grinning, Trinity imagined a cutie with pigtails and stubby nails who relentlessly teased her brothers and got away with it.

"So you spent the night together in the same room," she said, "set up all cozy before a fire like we are now."

"That's right. Except..." His hands dropped from cradling the back of his head and he angled more toward her. "Around midnight, the noises began."

"What noises?"

"Distant. Indistinct. But they grew louder. High-pitched, screeching sounds. Scratching on floorboards. Somewhere far off, a rooster crowed."

"At midnight?"

"That's when we woke our father. He'd drifted off, was snoring softly, but by this time Mom was hiding under the covers, too. He scolded us at first but when he heard the noises, I swear I saw his hair stand on end."

A shiver raced over her skin. Bringing up her legs, she hugged her knees. "What did he do?"

"What any father and husband would do in that kind of situation. He went to investigate. He was gone for what seemed like forever, and with every passing minute the sounds only swelled. That cock crowed again, nearer, louder. And the screeches seemed right there on top of us. The flapping of wings. Smells of a barnyard. A coop. I pulled the cover up over my head when an eerie clucking began."

"Clucking?"

"Right then our father returned. He told us not to worry. He'd found the problem. It was only a bunch of *poultry*-geists."

She gaped and then glared at the same time Zack broke into a grin. Two beats later, she let out the breath she'd been holding on a growl and slapped his arm. "That was so not funny."

"Ah, I was only egging you on."

A small smile cracked even as her eyes narrowed more. "Don't leave your day job." Poultry-geists, indeed.

"My older brothers have kids. When I go over they always want to hear that story. Entertainment I can do. Diaper duty I leave to the experts."

"Not daddy material?"

"As I'm sure you'd already guessed."

She shifted to lie down, propping herself up on her side. She'd like to know more about his family.

"How often do you see them?"

"Not including Christmas, Easter, birthdays and other numerous family occasions? All the time. I don't mind. They're good kids. What does irritate is—" His jaw tensed and he cut himself off.

She prodded. "What?"

"It's not important."

"I say it is."

He scrubbed his jaw. "Frankly I'm tired of hearing that I should settle down. Like it's Regency times and—" he put on an Oxford accent "—every gentleman must find a suitable wife."

"Maybe they just want to see you happy?"

His eyebrows knitted. "I don't look happy?"

"Happy in a *nonbachelor* way." She put it out there. "Your

family must feel like they're in a revolving door the number of times they see you with a new woman hanging off your arm."

"Good thing it's my life and not theirs." He leaned back, latched his fingers behind his head again and stared off at some distant point past the ceiling. "Unless you weren't aware, I'm content with my life just the way it is. What about you?"

"I'm busy, settled and happy with my job."

"And unattached after that breakup."

"Definitely unattached."

"But I'm guessing you'd want to tie a knot sometime…have children someday. You have a knack with babies."

Her heart dropped an inch and she looked into the fire. When she felt his expression sharpen, she explained. "I like children. Babies."

"That's kind of obvious."

Her cheeks began to burn, but she shouldn't feel awkward. Zack had his life and she had hers.

"Thing is," she said. "I don't have family to fall back on, and sometimes both a mother and father drop out of the picture, for one reason or another. I have friends," she went on. "Good friends. But no one I'd trust enough with a child of my own if something, you know, ever happened. And I have nothing against adoption. Heck, I would've loved to have been adopted by a loving family. And, when it's needed, I can't slight good foster care." She took a breath. "Life is about choices. I've chosen not to go down that having-my-own-children path."

Trinity took a breath and looked from the bed of flickering flames back to Zack.

A crease forming between his brows, he shifted and lay down on his side, too. Propped up on an arm, he set his jaw in the cup of that palm. After a curious moment of his intense gaze skewering hers, she shifted, too, and frowned.

"You mean not get married, have children?" he asked. "I thought you sacked the boyfriend because he didn't approve of kids?"

"That's right. He didn't approve of them at all. I mean, you might not want to be a father, but you like your nieces and nephews, don't you? You like this baby?"

"She can be noisy and smelly and has caused me a ton of worry. But sure I *like* her." He slanted his head and then nodded. "Who wouldn't?"

"I might not plan to have any of my own, but I couldn't spend my life with someone who thinks kids are a waste of space."

His lips twitched. "Bet he didn't like puppies, either."

"Or kittens."

Zack was kind enough to smile softly. "You were right to ditch him." Then he shifted and changed the subject. "What about your professional life?" he asked. "What are you working toward?"

"One day I hope to be the editor in chief of the biggest, glossiest magazine around. Basically world domination in my field." She added, "While staying clear of men who tell bad chicken jokes."

"No getting away from me tonight."

She put on a sigh. "Guess I'll suffer for a good cause."

The tease in his eyes gradually took on a vaguely different light at the same time the quirk lifting one side of his mouth faded away and a different awareness began to ripple between them. The crackle from the fire sounded louder, the rise and fall of his chest became deeper. Pumping in and out of the light, the pulse at the side of his throat throbbed faster and, entranced, her body responded to it all.

Her breasts came alive, swelling, heating. Low inside, a delicious ache flowered and grew. She watched his lips part slightly, saw his eyes darken more, then he reached out and a hot fingertip trailed her jaw. That delicious ache spread south— a sweet, raw burn.

When he brushed back hair fallen over her face and his hot palm stayed to cup her cheek, all the oxygen in the room disappeared. Suddenly heavy, her eyelids drifted shut as her body—her very essence—gravitated unerringly toward his. With the lights out, with this extraordinary man she barely knew, everything felt so unreal. So...*imminent*. She didn't want to think about who he really was. That before today she would have given him less than the time of day. At this moment, he truly was irresistible.

"Your hair," he said in a deep, drugging voice. "A wave came loose from its tie."

"Oh." She breathed in. Out. Then the words just slipped past her lips and she said it. "I thought you might've wanted to kiss me."

That pulse in his throat beat twice as hard and, while she held her breath, he blinked slowly once. "Actually I've wanted to do that all night." He leaned across and his mouth grazed hers, first slowly one way then the other. "Trouble is," he murmured, "if I kiss you now, I won't want to stop."

She quivered to her pom-pom-topped toes and clapped a hand over her scruples' eyes.

Who said anything about stopping?

But then her thoughts slid back to what had brought them here in the first place. "What about the baby?"

"You're right," he agreed even as his lidded eyes drifted shut. He leaned that inch closer and his mouth feathered over hers again. "We should think of our responsibilities."

But his mouth lingered and as his scent burrowed deeper, Trinity couldn't recall a single reason why she shouldn't fan her palm up over his shoulder and bring herself delectably, irreversibly closer. When he tasted the corner of her mouth—a deliberate, potent caress—that beautiful ache flooded her core and the last remnants of common sense shut down. She'd be lucky to remember her own name.

The tip of his tongue slid a deliberate line across the seam of her lips. "Maybe if we just snuggled?" he said and she felt his grin. "You know. To keep warm."

When his sandpaper chin grazed the side of her face and

he dropped a kiss on the shell of her ear, the knowledge—
the intense glow of longing—was too much. Near dizzy with
need, she told him in a husky voice, "I think snuggling would
be okay."

A big palm traced down her side. She heard a sigh—her
own—and then he was kissing her in earnest and with an in-
nate skill that left her reeling.

As his tongue penetrated and twined languidly with hers, everything but the ecstasy evaporated. His kiss was hot and deep
and thrilling. When his head angled down and body ironed up
against hers, she only surrendered more. His superior weight
eased her over and back until she lay flat beneath him.

With their mouths still locked, a satisfied noise rumbled in
his chest as one arm haloed her head and the other hand held
and gently directed her chin. Her splayed fingers found their
way over the broad dome of his back while her foot—its slip-
per now lost—dragged curling toes up his hard leg and her
hips pressed up longingly. She was drowning, dying in some
perfect wicked dream. When the kiss deepened more and he
ground against her, his arousal pressed into her belly and she
groaned and reached down.

A log crumpled and fell into its bed of hot ash. The hiss of
sparks flying brought her back with a start. When she turned
her head, broke the kiss, his head came up.

His breathing was labored and his heavy gaze uncommonly
dark. No hint of understanding or restraint marked in his expression. As he hovered above her, all she saw, and felt, was
resolve.

An audible rumble vibrated from his chest as his gaze lowered to devour her lips and his head gradually dropped again.
Uncertain, Trinity held herself still. She'd gotten carried away,
too, but did she really want to make love to a man she was
supposed to despise—particularly with a baby sleeping a few
feet away?

His parted lips stopped a hairbreadth from hers. The walls

receded as she swallowed deeply and the ground seemed to sink away beneath her. Then, on a real growl, he clenched his jaw and rolled away. Trinity's heart fell at the same instant her throat clogged with a dozen different emotions. He was disappointed. Frustrated. She was sorry she'd led him on, if that's what had happened, but he'd just have to deal with the sting of rejection like most of the population.

Then a powerful arm scooped under her shoulders and Trinity's heart skipped two beats as he drew her mercilessly near, half on top of him. His body was beyond hard, as if a thousand steel links had locked him into place. She felt vulnerable, still wanting him, but also a thousand times decided. She might be physically attracted to him, more than she'd been to any man, but she hadn't come here for sex. And she intended to leave this house with that assertion intact. Regret lasted longer than pleasure.

She was about to tell him again—*no*—but as that tense moment passed into another, he didn't try to kiss her again. He simply lay there, stiff on his back, his arm holding her close, fingers beginning to drift up and down the silk of her sleeve.

"Does this qualify as snuggling?" he asked.

"Put me back down and I'll tell you."

He considered it then eased her over until she lay beside him. Resting on an elbow, his cheek balanced in a palm, he gazed down at her. "We should probably get some sleep."

"That's a good idea."

He nodded and when his arm reached under and brought her gently over, she didn't resist. Making love might be out of the question, but she wasn't made of stone. What harm could come from cuddling with a man-god on a chilly night?

As her cheek gradually lowered to rest against the hard plateau of his T-shirt-covered chest, Trinity let out a long end-of-the-day breath, listened to his heart thumping like he'd run a mile and closed her eyes. She was almost asleep when a thought struck and her eyes flew open.

Damn it. She'd never made that call to New York.

Four

The next morning, Zack blinked open his eyes long before either of his guests.

Beyond that south wall of windows, snow was still falling and all was buried in a deep sea of white. He'd need a shovel to make it much past the front door. Sure bet, roads were impassable. Child Services wouldn't be out today. Which meant it was just him, the baby and Trinity Matthews...who, despite her qualms, had slept right alongside him the entire night.

Remembering her peaceful, even breathing, the alluring warmth of her skin, he carefully edged over to face her...then didn't move for the longest time.

Both hands were clasped on the pillow under her chin as if she were in prayer. A sweep of sable hair fell like a stole around one shoulder's vibrant red silk. Long, curved eyelashes rested against healthy, flushed cheeks. Her lips were pink, slightly parted and near irresistible.

Yesterday, after they'd learned the Dales were out, that same mouth had been set, determined; she'd wanted to turn back.

Later, cradling the baby as if the little girl was her own, her lips had been lifted in a perpetual, caring smile. Last night, those same lips had glistened in the firelight, tempting him to take them. Take her.

He wanted her still.

Zack sucked down a breath. His blood was pumping faster, hotter, and the longer he laid here and dwelled, the harder and more on edge he'd get. He wanted to sift his fingers through that long, silken hair. Longed to gather her close and claim that second kiss. So warm and honeyed, he could taste her now…

Biting down, he moved the quilt back and a moment later ten bare toes were curling into the soft pile rug which had formed the base for their campout bed. Stretching his back, he glanced around. The fire had burned out, and the light over the bar hadn't blinked back on. Electricity was still out, which meant no power for the landline. Too late to wish he'd had that generator replaced after it had died last year.

He dashed a look over at the kitchen counter.

Had his cell regained reception?

He tiptoed over and tried to thumb the phone on. Still no reception. But the blank screen sparked a thought and he frowned. Trinity had good reason for not making it to New York this morning, but she ought to have at least texted when she'd had the chance. That "five minutes" had turned into the rest of the night.

Knowing Trinity's history—how she'd grown up a ward of the state—he better understood her decision to stay until the baby's situation was resolved. With no Mrs. Dale, thank God she *had* insisted. He couldn't have handled the mess, the crying and constant soothing that an infant seemed to need. As far as those kinds of occupations went, he was a giant dud. He was a bachelor, unencumbered and unattached. For the foreseeable future, he planned to keep it that way.

His family laughed about it, said he'd change his attitude when the right woman came along, but Zack wasn't so sure.

He enjoyed his freedom too much. And being the odd one out as far as starting his own family was concerned certainly had its advantages. His brothers were good businessmen but their first loyalty was to their immediate families. Which left *him* to tighten any company slack that from time to time crept in.

Everyone had an ultimate role to fill. Clearly taking over from his father, being chairman of Harrison Hotels, was his. Although folk who read trashy magazines—or wrote for them—might mistake him for little more than a self-centered womanizer.

A shiver raced over his skin and he studied the fireplace again. He should light another log but he wouldn't risk the noise. Then again, the baby hadn't made a peep for—he checked his wristwatch—ten straight hours.

Padding back over, he hunkered down.

Her little arms were out of the wrap. Her cheeks were pink. He'd never seen a more angelic face. She might have been a porcelain doll except for the slight rise and fall of her chest. Trinity had mentioned saying goodbye would be hard.

A corner of his mouth hitched up.

She sure is a sweetheart.

His stomach muscles tensed and he pushed to his feet. Hunger pains. With no dinner last night, he really ought to eat.

He was standing in the kitchen, hands on hips, wondering how quietly he could set coffee on the stove when his cell buzzed. The realization sank in—reception was back—and he dived at the counter. Striding down the back hall, he waited until he was in the study to answer.

"Snowstorm, anyone?"

At the voice, Zack relaxed. Not Child Services but Thomas, his younger brother, a regular smart aleck and the sibling he felt closest to. Zack clicked the door shut.

"I'm about to get out the snowplow," Zack joked.

"Mmm. Sounds like fun."

Remembering his guests asleep in the living room, Zack

crossed to a window view of winter wonderland in April and pressed a palm against the jamb. "It's not as bad as all that."

"Surrounded by wilderness. Cut off from society. Give me downtown traffic and Starbucks any day."

"Don't mention coffee. Haven't had this morning's hit yet."

"Then I'll keep it brief. Dad wants to know how it went on that deal yesterday with James Dirkins. When can we expect to close?"

Zack's arm fell from the jamb. "I need more time." The line crackled. When Thomas's words cut in and out, Zack clamped the phone harder to his ear. "What was that?"

"I said I'm sure Dad's happy to leave the negotiations to you. Where business is concerned, you can make a porcupine quill go down as smooth as Jell-O."

Admittedly, he was a good negotiator. Success was about keeping emotion out of the mix. A cool head was key. Still…

He remembered Dirkins's expression yesterday—drawn, reflective…reluctant to hand over his deceased son's inheritance—and for some reason, an image of Trinity holding the baby flashed into his mind's eye.

His stomach rolling again, Zack shrugged.

"James Dirkins has a strong personal attachment to the place. I get that."

"Uh, *sorry?* Since when did personal matters ever factor into your corporate dealings?"

Zack's eyebrows snapped together. "Since never. I was just saying."

Silence echoed down the line.

"Are you all right, Zack? You sound…different."

"I'm good. Better than good." He crossed the room and opened the door a crack. He thought he'd heard the baby. "Tell Dad I'll have the papers signed this week," he said, cocking an ear and peering out down the hall.

Out in the living room, the baby squeaked.

"Zack, do you have someone with you?"

"Uh-huh."

"A female?"

"Two." He thought he heard Thomas drop the phone. Before the questions could fly, he cut his brother off. "It's a long story."

"For this, I have a few minutes."

Grinning, he headed out. "Sorry, buddy. Gotta go."

Zack found Trinity still sound asleep and the baby lying quietly, looking as if she were waiting for someone to notice she was finally awake. When he bent closer, she caught the movement and focused. The vibrant blue of her eyes took him a little off guard, but when she continued to stare, he tried a small smile. Waited.

She didn't smile back.

However, neither did she burst into tears, although her brow seemed somehow to pinch as if she were uncomfortable. Zack scrubbed his chin. Must be tough not being able to roll. Maybe he could shift her a little, prop her up. Gingerly he scooped a hand beneath her back and instantly recoiled. Oh, God, she was *wet*. Make that sopping, right through her outfit. Shuddering, he glanced across. Trinity was still out of it.

Studying the baby again, he whispered, "So what am I supposed to do with you?"

She only stared, her little fingers wiggling on top of the blanket.

He scratched his temple, paced away then back again. He couldn't bear to think of her lying in those sodden clothes, and yet he couldn't imagine handling them to change her, either. Every man had his limit and this was his.

Placing thatched fingers on his head, he thought for a long moment. Then he cleared his throat. Not on purpose. Not really.

While the baby only looked harder as though he were some kind of puzzle, Trinity sucked in a breath and, gradually waking, stretched tall one arm. Two seconds later, she sat bolt upright, her violet eyes round and startled. Her gaze found his at the same time she shoved a fall of hair back and held it from her face.

"It wasn't a dream."

He rocked on his heels. "Nope. We're real. And *she's* wet."

Trinity slapped the quilt away and crawled over. As if the baby knew "the one with the bottle" was near, she screwed up her nose and mewed out something that might have been a small cry.

Hands going to her cheeks, Trinity visibly melted. "Oh, poor darling. She must be hungry."

"There's a more pressing matter."

"She needs changing."

"Oh, yeah."

"You don't want to have a go?"

"I could answer that question a number of ways but the conclusions would all be the same."

She pretended to be surprised. "No?"

"I'm a man who can admit to his shortcomings."

"A shortcoming implies that you'd like to better yourself and learn."

"Then I used the wrong word."

Grinning and shaking her head, Trinity stood to collect the baby.

He'd seen her in the same pajamas last night but now, in the bright morning light rather than flickering shadows, he received the full impact. The shirt and bottoms literally hung off her slender frame. Not a suggestion of a curve or line anywhere. The trousers were so long, they puddled around her feet, the sleeves hung past her fingertips, the front was buttoned as high as it would go…and, hands down, it was the sexiest set of ladies' nightwear Zack had ever seen.

Stepping back to give her room, his attention was drawn to her face, pillow creased on one side but well rested and already, within a moment of waking, fully animated. As she smiled at the baby, her eyes captured the morning light, which sent them sparkling like a pair of cut amethyst. If he weren't careful, a man could get hypnotized by eyes like that.

When she lifted the baby up from the recliner, however, reality struck a blow. He heard—almost *felt*—the squelch and he backed up more, all the way to the kitchen.

"I'll handle the formula."

Trinity was rubbing her nose with the baby's. "I might give her a bath. Freshen her up. Want to help?"

"After I finish bottle duty—sure thing."

No censuring look this time. She merely drifted off with her bundle toward the laundry room. The way she was grinning and babbling to the baby, she'd forgotten all about her fatigue the previous night and was ready to do it all over again. Great because, unless he was mistaken, more of the same was precisely what was in store this coming day.

Zack waited to hear splashing from the laundry room then happy squeals before placing the formula canister on the counter. Clearly Trinity loved caring for the baby, which meant regardless of her teasing he was off the hook as far as hands-on went. And, seriously, no one wanted the poor kid to burst into tears the moment he took over, least of all him.

A few minutes later, finished with the bottle preparation and curious, he moved into the laundry room. Trinity was drawing the baby out from the tub, laying her on a towel she'd spread on the counter. The front of her pj's were wet. Strands of hair, too. But with her sleeves rolled up to the elbow, she either didn't notice or didn't care, and Zack wondered. What usually made Trinity this happy? Who were her friends? Where did she live in New York? Maybe they'd passed each other on the street. Had caught the same elevator.

But the bigger question was: What was in store for them this evening? He'd displayed mammoth restraint last night. When he'd whipped her over, damn near on top of him, with her breasts through that silk pressed against him and her parted lips so close and tempting, he was still amazed he'd been able to bring his rabid testosterone levels down so quickly. But he'd never forced a lady into anything and had no intention of starting now. He didn't have to. He'd made up his mind and whenever that happened—whether in the corporate world or the bedroom—the game was as good as won. He'd been gentle on Ms. Matthews up to this point. But when the baby went down tonight, he'd work it so Trinity couldn't consider the word *no.* She wasn't the only one who knew the meaning of resolve.

Carefully drying the baby's damp, fair curls, Trinity noticed him standing behind her. Her smile flashed wider, white and warm.

"Just in time. Want to shake on some baby powder?"

His stomach kicked. "On the baby?"

"I can powder myself so, yes, the baby."

He handed over the talc bottle. "You did such a good job last time."

She shook powder on her palm before patting the white substance pretty much all over the child then reached for an undershirt. Zack cocked his head. It was ridiculously small. Then again, so were those limbs. The way Trinity maneuvered the baby's head then arms through those tiny openings had Zack biting his lip. The one time he'd tried a similar feat with his firstborn nephew, he'd worried he might snap something. Too delicate. Too difficult. And yet Trinity made it look easy.

"Are you sure you haven't done this before?"

She hesitated a heartbeat. "A friend gave birth a couple of years back," she said, reaching for a clean diaper. "I helped with bits here and there."

"You were never worried you might accidentally let her slide off the counter or prick her with a pin?"

"Well, sure, you have to be careful."

She lifted the baby's bottom and slid the diaper underneath. She had the outfit paradigms worked out, too, slipping snug cuffs and sleeves over those teensy fists, one of which the baby had been busy sucking. Now, interrupted, she let out a little cry while those gorgeous blue eyes filled with tears. Zack dragged a hand down his face. He hated to see her upset. How did parents stand this kind of stuff full-time? Then again some fathers didn't. If his dad had been around more for this kind of thing in those early years, perhaps his parents' marriage wouldn't be going through the problems it was now. The Harrison kids loved their time away with their father in Colorado once a year, but their mom had needed more from her husband. Unfortunately, his father had realized too late.

When the numerous snaps were pressed shut, Trinity lifted the baby and cradled her close. "Is the bottle ready?"

"I'll make sure it's still warm," he said, striding out.

A moment later, Trinity walked into the kitchen and he stopped shaking the nipple over his wrist. After dropping a kiss to the whimpering baby's brow, she asked, "Shall we assume positions?"

He held up the bottle. "Torpedo ready."

She moved to the recliner. "Lowering into position."

Seated, she took the bottle. A perfect landing was made and that lulling quiet, interspersed with the sound of suckling, again reigned supreme.

As the baby drank, Zack quietly pulled over his usual dining room chair and, at a safe distance, settled down to watch. When the bottle was half-empty, it dawned; he should have been bored. Surely any novelty had worn off by now. No way would he sit around to watch any other infant feed, and yet here he was absorbed in every movement.... How her baby blues grew drowsier, the way her fingers squeezed the bottle like a kitten padding a soft blanket.

Then again, it wasn't as if he could go turn on the sports or catch up on the news on his laptop, which was out of battery. If he had other things to do, he'd be off doing them.

He was about to suggest a burp when Trinity eased the bottle away and brought the baby upright. In a blink he was back with a hand towel. *Please, Lord, let there be no horrific spit-*

ting up this time. After a moment or two rubbing, the baby rewarded them by bringing up a decent amount of wind. Zack let out that breath. Good girl!

Trinity settled farther back into the lounge chair. "Hey, we're really getting the hang of this."

Zack's chest puffed out, too, but, of course, she was speaking to the baby. Those two were the team. He was merely the runner. Which was a novelty. Usually he was the one in the driver's seat. At the office, he called the shots and others listened. In relationships, he set the tone and parameters or he didn't call again. He liked to get along but it needed to be on his terms. That's how he'd managed to stay successful, as well as single. A combination that served him well.

"I've been thinking."

Dragging his gaze away from her lips, Zack brought himself back. "What's that?"

"Would it be wrong to give her a name while we're taking care of her? It doesn't feel right calling her 'baby' all the time."

"What did you have in mind?"

"What girls' names do you like?"

He went blank. "I've never thought about it."

"Do traditional ones appeal? Emily, Molly, Beatrice?"

"Maybe I'm more New Age."

"Brook, Fallon, Mira." She lowered the baby and set the nipple back in her mouth. "Maybe Summer or Skye to go with her eyes."

Something clicked and he sat straighter.

"I like Bonnie," he said.

"Pardon?"

"'Bonnie Blue Eyes.' It's a song." His father used to sometimes sing it.

Her gaze lowered to the baby again and she smiled, softer and more telling than ever. "I like it, too."

And he liked the way Trinity held her lip between her teeth when she was pleased. The way her eyes lit and throat made that cute humming sound. Hell, he even liked the way she rarely cut him an inch, sniping about past affairs and business decisions, neither of which she knew anything concrete about.

Zack blinked and felt his brow furrow.

Too much reflection. Maybe he was coming down with a strain of cabin fever.

He crossed to the fireplace and while he selected a log from the stack, she asked, "Does your cell have service this morning?"

"I got a call," he said, finding the matches, "just before you two woke up."

"Child Services?" Her voice sounded hopeful but also a little troubled.

"I'm sure the baby will be in good hands when she leaves us."

"I'd just love to know her story. What happened to her mother."

Same. But they couldn't do anything about that right now. Settling that log in the fire, he changed the subject.

"My brother Thomas called."

"The youngest. The one who shot out of the haunted barn's bedroom first when the light went out."

"He went on to become a track-and-field star in school."

Trinity laughed, a light, musical sound that seemed to fill the room, so different to her kitten attempts at a growl.

"Was he checking on how you were holding up in this weather?" she asked.

"That, as well as seeing how I was coming along with a business transaction. We're negotiating to buy the Dirkins hotel."

The penny dropped. "So *that's* why you were there yesterday afternoon," she said. "To seal the deal."

"We're not there yet." He struck the match. "The owner's holding out for more."

"Fair enough."

"Except the hotel's not worth any more. There's a swag of

renovations needed. Updated plumbing and a sheltered fore-court for starters."

"Maybe he won't sell."

"He'll sell. He just needs more time. He's thinking with his heart at the moment, not his head."

"Heaven forbid."

"Only if you want to succeed in business." Even when it was understandable. He prodded at the weak flames, coaxing them to grow. "James Dirkins built that place himself in the seven-ties. He'd wanted to pass it down to his son."

"What's changed?"

Zack set the poker aside. "His son died recently—tragically, I'm afraid."

He heard her gasp and imagined her clinging to the baby—to Bonnie—extra tight.

"Poor man," she said. "Of course he'd be thinking with his heart. Leave him alone. What's one more piece of real estate to you?"

She was always so ready to jump on his back. "Dirkins con-tacted us, not the other way round. A year after the accident, he wants to move on. I want to be the one to buy."

She looked down as she mulled that over. "Because of your attachment to this area?"

"Partly."

"Isn't that thinking with your heart?"

With flames eating into the log now, he drew to his feet. "Clever, but it's not the same."

"If you say so."

His grin held no humor. "Sure, I like this location, but I only go into a venture if I'm certain of its viability."

And if he ended up offering a little more than the hotel was worth, his decision would be based on future returns not sen-timent. That kind of attitude got you in trouble. Lines were blurred, misjudgments made. He wouldn't forget the time, many years ago now, when he'd bought a car from a friend who'd needed the cash. He'd paid too much and hadn't cared until the vehicle died a week later. The rings had been gummed up using an oil additive to stop the exhaust from blowing smoke and the engine from ultimately packing it in. The sense of betrayal—of being duped because of attachments, because of trust—had been far worse than any money wasted.

Now Zack took another clearer look at Trinity and the baby and headed for his study.

Levelheaded. That's the way he was, the way he needed to stay. He was only thankful that sex could be uncomplicated. Someone else could deal with heartstrings.

Five

An hour later, returning to the living room from fitting Bonnie with a fresh diaper, Trinity stopped in her tracks.

Seemed Zack had grown tired of his own company and had prowled out from his study, where he'd holed up since their conversation about James Dirkins earlier. But now sorting through paperwork at the dining table, he only flicked her a cursory glance, a brief smile, before collecting his coffee and draining the cup. When she stayed put, wondering again why he'd disappeared the way he had—why he seemed so cool toward her now—he finally met her gaze.

His lidded eyes were dark. A lock of finger-combed strong black hair hung over his brow. She'd never seen a sexier sight than Zack at this moment, somehow managing to loll in a straight-back chair, his jaw bristled with morning stubble. His look was so sultry, lazy and hot—in a heartbeat, she was reliving the scolding heat of desire he'd brought out in her the previous night.

She'd ached to take their embrace to the next level. Falling asleep against his hard heat had almost been compensation enough. She'd felt vulnerable and yet inexplicably safe. Which was a feat in itself. Trust wasn't her strong suit, and to think she'd felt it with Mr. Loose and Lucky here.

"Do you need something?" he asked.

"I figure I'd better call the office and let my boss know I won't be in."

Kate Illis was a fair but strong boss. To survive in business these days, a person had to be tough. Kate had placed her chips on Trinity Matthews when she could have backed other, some might say, more talented writers. Her catch phrase was: *find a way.*

Needless to say Kate would not be pleased with this wrench in the works. But even now, gazing down at baby Bonnie, Trinity couldn't regret her decision to stay. Life was full of choices. Sometimes a person needed to put herself out on a limb. Bonnie had needed someone. And if her parents were permanently out of the picture for whatever reason, she'd need *someone* even more.

Zack was saying, "...should let them know you might not make it in tomorrow, either."

She frowned. "You really don't think anyone will be able to get in?"

"Or out."

Rotating in the chair, he scanned the view through the window. The snow was still falling, growing deeper, it seemed, by the minute. Not for one moment had she thought she'd be in Zack's company more than a couple of hours, and yet it seemed likely they'd have to put up with each other at least another day. He was the one who'd insisted they stay here and despite what she thought of him—what she'd read—she had to admit that he'd been patient and, in his own way, helpful. However, given his current detached demeanor, it seemed that patience might be running thin. The novelty must be wearing off. He wanted his own space back and, on a baser level, she got that. Normally, she liked her own space, too.

With the cooing baby in her arms, she crossed over and let him know. "I'm sorry you have to put up with me this long."

His brows knitted then he exhaled. Almost smiled. "Trinity, I'm glad you're here."

She brightened. "Really?"

"No way would I have managed alone with diapers and burping and all that rocking."

She deflated again. He might have come on to her last night—probably out of Don Juan habit—but his real interest in her was clear. She recalled his expression of near horror this morning when she'd lifted diaper-drenched Bonnie into her arms. In so many ways, he was a "strong, capable male" but not when it came to baby business. As long as Bonnie was here under his roof, he needed her. Couldn't have managed without her. But once the baby was gone...

He was glad she was here?

She feigned a casual shrug. "Guess you owe me one."

His eyes flashed and a ghost of that familiar mischievous smile touched his lips. "And how do you suggest I pay?"

She let her imagination fly. "Oh, how about a long, decadent vacation somewhere sandy and warm? No snow."

"Colorful cocktails 24/7?" he asked, finding his feet and moving closer.

"With entertainment when I want it and only the lull of rolling waves when I don't."

"Are you partial to a massage or two?" he asked, circling slowly around her.

With the baby's weight dragging on her shoulders, she confessed, "I'd adore a massage."

From behind, smooth, low words brushed her ear. "With clothes or without?"

A surprise rush of heat filled her core. She had to concentrate to brace her legs to keep her knees from caving in. Was it his sultry tone, the provocative question or the sumptuous image of his big hands sliding over her well-oiled body that left her every inch burning for attention?

"We have a resort in the Bahamas." His breath was warm against her crown now. "What would you say to a long week-end?"

She tried to laugh it off. "I wasn't serious."

His chin grazed her temple. "Let me know the moment you are."

Her legs turned to water and, eyes drifting shut again, she swayed. Guess his mood was improving. It was all she could do not to pivot around, wind her arms around his neck and bring her suddenly hungry mouth to his. Of course, there was the baby to consider. But what about tonight?

When all was quiet and Bonnie had been put to bed, she was certain he would try to kiss her again. And if the caress was anything like the scorching moments they'd already shared...

But then reality struck again. Zack was bored, edgy. He was only filling in time the way he might with any woman he found attractive. No matter what he said, what he did or what he offered, she needed to remember that her being here was primarily a convenience.

Composed again, she told him, "I should make that call."

She felt his considering pause for a heart-pumping moment before the warmth of his body at her back evaporated. With a fluid gait, he crossed over to the table and, broad shoulders squared, lowered himself into the same chair he'd been sitting in.

"If your cell doesn't have reception," he said, collecting a document to peruse, "feel free to try mine."

She acknowledged the offer with a polite nod before going into the living room to set the baby down in her recliner. Her eyes bright, her darling expression content, Bonnie didn't make a squeak. Trinity cupped her crown for a moment—so soft and warm—before asking, "Do you mind looking after her? This call should only take a minute."

His head flew up from his work then his jaw shifted to one side. "What if she cries?"

"Panic?"

While Zack's face lost a little of its color, grinning, Trinity made her way to the bedroom where she'd stowed her belongings. She wasn't worried the baby would cry, and if she did, despite his claims, Zack would cope. And if he *didn't* cope, well, help was two seconds away. This call had to be made, and she wanted complete focus when she and Kate spoke.

In the privacy of that room, Trinity turned her cell on, and noted the bars. After filling her lungs, she dialed. Typically efficient, Kate answered on the second ring.

"Something wrong, Trin?"

"A little hitch. I won't be in today. Probably not tomorrow, either."

"Are you ill?"

"Stuck in Colorado."

"Ah, the snow. I skimmed something about the crazy weather out that way. So your flight was canceled?"

Trinity's stomach swooped. She couldn't lie. Honesty went hand in hand with respect. Kate deserved the truth.

"I missed my flight, but for a very good reason." She explained about waiting for a cab, finding the baby, needing to stay until she was in the right hands. "But snow's still falling, the power's off and I can't see the authorities getting out to collect Bonnie before tomorrow."

"Stop there. Who's Bonnie?"

"The baby."

"I didn't think you knew her."

"I don't. It's just she has these amazing blue eyes and we both agreed the name suited her."

"*Both* agreed? You mean someone at the hotel. I'm confused."

"Actually I'm staying at a private address, a cabin a bit out of town."

"You don't know anyone in Colorado."

"Zack was in the cab when we found her."

"So you're staying in the woods with a man you hadn't met before yesterday? I hope he's a gentleman."

Trinity nibbled her lower lip. "Most of the time."

"Okay. Now I'm *worried*."

"Don't be. I'm here of my own free will."

"I see." A pause. "Does this man happen to be good-looking?"

"That has nothing to do with—"

"Is he hot or not?"

Trinity sighed. "He's hot." *Scorching, as a matter of fact.*

"So who is this guy?"

She might as well admit to it. "Zack Harrison of Harrison Hotels."

Silence ensued, followed by a long, low whistle. "New York's most eligible bachelor. Looks, wealth, charisma and…"

"And a reputation as an amoral womanizer who'd sell his grandmother to seal a deal." Kate was preaching to the converted.

"A real devil in disguise," her boss confirmed, "and the girls line up for miles to be prodded by his pitchfork. Not that you'd be that stupid."

Trinity's chest tightened. Kate didn't need to know about her slip. That kiss. Those terrible urges. She schooled her voice.

"His reputation has nothing to do with what's happening here."

"Good God, of course not. Must be hard being in the same room with a man whose only concerns are for his own bottom line. Closing that community center to use the land for up-market high-rises. Has he mentioned anything about his Colorado deal?"

She was talking about that hotel Zack wanted to buy? The

one whose owner's only son recently had passed away. Shivering, Trinity hugged herself. She knew where her boss was going with this.

"Kate, I couldn't put in print anything I heard off the record here."

"You know I admire your ethics. I'd just love to know how anyone gets through life without a conscience. Slapping a base offer on the table is one thing. Publicly blaming the poor man for his own son's death as a way to wear him and the price down even more is shameless."

Trinity was left gaping. She'd heard nothing of that story until now, and she found it hard to believe, even of Zack. But wasn't she being naive? Zack Harrison was known for his ruthless dealings. Because he'd shown a sliver of compassion and had brought that baby home didn't change his history.

Kate was saying she'd look after that interview scheduled for today and her other line was ringing. She had to go.

After promising to call in again, Trinity disconnected but she hung back returning to the lounge. She needed time to gather her thoughts. So much had happened since yesterday afternoon when she jumped in that cab.

A devil in disguise...

From the moment she'd laid eyes on Zack, she'd known women would fall at his feet. He oozed sex appeal and the kind of self-confidence that females flocked to and other men admired. Most likely he'd lost count of the notches carved on his bedposts around the country. The world. The Bahamas, for instance?

Her eyes prickling with emotion, she tossed the cell on the bed.

She must have been dreaming to have felt so safe in his arms last night.

While Trinity took care of that phone call and the baby relaxed in her chair, Zack finally cracked, slapped down a Har-

rison's L.A. restaurant refurbishment quote on the table then
shot a glance into every corner of the room. Last night's retell-
ing of his famed chicken-ghost story was not playing games
with his head. That squeaky scratching was real and getting
louder by the second.

Zack found his feet.

Where the hell was it coming from?

As he focused his every sense on the sound, a disquieting
sensation funneled through his center. Yesterday he'd scoffed at
Trinity's suggestion of kidnappers…abductors. But this minute,
more than ever, he wondered about their baby's background.
Well cared for, provisions supplied… Was she abandoned or
had she been stolen? Perhaps by someone who'd ended up with
cold feet, lucky for her.

Fingers flexing at his sides, Zack crossed to the wall of windows then, senses tingling, he leaned close to scan the appar-
ent quiet outside. Drifts still slanted in from a gray churning
sky. All the world was buried in a deep blanket of white. No
sign of life anywhere. And yet that infernal scratching kept on.

He was about to grab a jacket—and his trusty baseball bat—
when something leaped out of the swirls and at windows—at
him. His thumping heart shot like a bullet up the back of his
throat at the same time his brain registered rows of teeth, yellow eyes, a hairy, pointed snout.

A wolf?

A heartbeat later, from a pillow of white, the culprit bounded
up again and tipping forward, Zack got a better look. Not a wolf
but a domestic dog—a *big* one. A mix of every gigantic canine
ever bred. Behind the woolly frame, a saber of a tail cut back
and forth across the snow.

It was the dog the Dales had inherited from an elderly rela-
tive. With his owners away, he must have wandered off from
the shelter of his gigantic doghouse and got lost in the storm
last night. Clearly he wanted to be friends…to play.

No one could stay out in that weather, but what disasters

would that lashing tail and mammoth body bring if let loose inside? Meaning to or not, his weight could knock Trinity flying, never mind the baby. Maybe he could lock him in the garage....

"Who's that?"

Zack glanced over his shoulder. Still in those baggy, sexy red pajamas, Trinity was back. He took a moment to reacquaint himself with her sparkling eyes, those tempting lips—the slight frown on her brow?—before focusing again on Fido. What was that dog's name?

"He belongs to the Dales," Zack said before Trinity could ask.

"He looks friendly."

"And huge."

"He must be cold."

Zack took in the natural fur coat. "He's well insulated."

"We can't just leave him out there. Bet he's hungry."

The dog bounced up and down, leaving a growing crater in the snow while Zack contemplated their dwindling supplies. "I'm not sure I have enough for his entrée."

"You're not going to leave him out there?"

"I wouldn't, except... Well, hell—he's a *mountain*."

"A *cold* mountain."

The dog licked the window, one long, upward swipe that left a noteworthy smear, and wagged his tail more.

Collecting the baby, Trinity pushed out a breath. "Are you going to let him in or am I?"

Zack looked back at Trinity and at the baby and rubbed the back of his neck. This place was getting crowded. "Maybe we should ask if the pigeons want to come in for cookies and tea?" But Trinity only rolled her eyes. "I'm just saying, he's *big*."

"So's this house. But, I suppose if you can stand to watch him shaking out there knee-deep while we sit in front of that gorgeous warm fire..."

Zack locked his arms over his chest and shook his head. This was not a good idea, even with Bonnie peering out the windows and making mumbled noises past the fist stuck in her mouth, like she wanted to meet this energetic new visitor. Like if she could have anything in the world, it would be to have a dog.

That dog.

Throwing up his arms, Zack headed out, muttering, "I'll let him in through the laundry room."

A moment later, he fanned back the door. The dog was waiting right there, tail still, one paw raised, wanting to shake hands. When Zack was young, the family had a dog, a Labrador that reminded him a little of this guy. He'd thought once or twice recently about getting a boxer or some such, but his Fifth Avenue apartment wasn't the place for a canine, and he didn't get out here enough to consider that option.

Shivering against the icy breeze, Zack put those thoughts aside and stepped back.

He let the mutt know, "We're letting the cold in."

When the dog merely cocked his head, Zack clicked his fingers and waved him in. The dog's face seemed to break into a smile before he shook out his coat. Zack shielded himself while specks of snow flew in every direction. Looking like a multi-colored mop now, this most recent guest padded in and lumbered past his reluctant host. Watching his rump and shaggy tail disappear through the doorway, Zack groaned. Guess there was one more for lunch. He took another look outside, just in case anyone else was lurking around, then closed the door and followed puddle tracks back to the living room.

The dog was sitting quiet and erect at Trinity's feet, his flap ears pinned back on his golden head. He was so still, he could've been set in cement. In contrast, Trinity was sighing her adoration. The way she clutched the baby high, shoulders hitched and smile wide, anyone would think she was six and had just met Santa Claus.

As Zack came closer, he could admit the dog's eyes were a merry kind of brown. He gave off a happy, easy vibe. He remembered Mrs. D telling him how protective and loyal he was.

That she trusted him with the grandkids. With any child. Well, fine. Just as long as he kept that sword of a tail in line.

Trinity reached down to ruffle the dog's damp crown. His tail thumped on the wooden floor and echoed through the rafters. "He's *gorgeous!*"

"He's wet."

"We'll get him settled before the fire, poor thing. If you hold the baby, I'll towel him down."

Zack was already marching back to the laundry room. He wanted to control some of the hair that would no doubt fly. "*I'll* towel him down."

"It's good to support someone when they need it," she called after him.

He pulled up at the doorway and digested her tone. "He's a *dog,*" he said, bending to grab towels from a cabinet.

"Dogs. People. Business associates."

Collecting two towels, he stopped. What the hell was she talking about?

He spun around and, caught off guard, jumped a foot in the air. That blasted dog had followed him, was standing right in front of him, panting, looking like he'd found a new best friend. Then he barked, once—loud. Zack pulled in his chin.

"You have some kind of attachment disorder?"

The tail started to thump.

With the dog close behind, Zack moved back to the living room, set a bath sheet before the fire and unraveled the other, ready to dry off that voluminous coat. He looked hard at Trinity, who was swaying back and forth, Bonnie in her arms, like nothing was out of the ordinary. At first glance, she looked happy enough but her jaw was tight, her usually plump lips pulled into a line, and he got the distinct impression she was avoiding eye contact. Guess the call with her boss hadn't gone so well.

Maybe she'd gotten the sack.

He hunkered down to dry the dog's coat. One small blessing… He didn't smell. Zack dropped the towel over the dog's head and rubbed.

"Did you get through to New York?" he asked.

"Uh-huh."

"Your boss not pleased?"

"She was remarkably understanding."

He rubbed along the dog's back. "Then what's the problem?"

"No problem."

"You sure?"

"Don't I look like I'm sure?"

Zack studied her frosty stare then shook out his towel and hair went flying. *Damn it*.

It was his experience that women liked to talk, which didn't always translate into them meaning what was said. He got the distinct impression Trinity wanted to tell him something that, through no fault of his own, he couldn't grasp and might not want to particularly hear anyway.

Without being asked, the dog rolled over onto his back, legs in the air. Zack quickly smothered a grin. "Just don't get too comfortable."

This was only temporary. This was *all* only temporary.

Trinity sat on the arm of the nearest recliner. "Looks like a great family dog."

"Did you have a dog growing up?"

"No. But I always wanted one."

"We had one." He rubbed the dog's belly and one hind leg began to kick.

"Did you take him to puppy school and for lots of walks?"

"I was too busy, shooting hoops, kicking balls or studying."

"You've always been competitive."

"I was motivated."

"Ever thought about sitting back on your laurels rather than pushing all the time?"

He looked over. There was that tone again and those gorgeous eyes were sparkling like she was angry. Upset. At him? Wondering, he kept drying.

"You mean take a backseat with my father's company?" He nudged the dog's ribs and he rolled back over. "Too much to learn. At some stage someone has to take over the reins."

"The reins of Harrison Hotels. And that's you. Mr. Ruthless."

Zack set his teeth. Now *he* was upset. "I'm not interested in labels."

"Yeah. I got that. What do your brothers and sister say about you taking possession of the crown?"

"Sienna has her own life. Off backpacking around Europe."

"Backpacking? With the Harrison money and connections, why not five stars all the way?"

"She's the rebel. Wants to do things her way, in her own time?"

Her head slanted and she smiled. "I think I'd like her."

Everyone did. "The guys have their families."

"And dogs, I suppose."

His stomach muscles tightened. *Enough.* He set down the towel and pushed to his feet. "Have I missed something? You're edgy and not because I thought twice about letting King Kong here into my house."

She shrugged. "He's obviously harmless."

"Don't avoid the question."

"There's nothing wrong."

Her exasperated *get off my back* expression didn't impress. He dropped the towel and sauntered over. "What happened during that phone call to New York?"

"I told you—"

"Not everything."

"I told Kate the story. She was surprised but understood. We talked about the weather, about you—"

"What about me?"

"That you have…a reputation."

"We established that. What else?"

Her slim nostrils flared then she released a breath. "That she needed to hear from me later in the day."

"Or no job?"

"Something like that."

He studied her wide, glistening eyes. *What are you hiding?*

He took another step closer. An instant later, the dog knocked the back of Zack's leg on his way to plunking himself down between them both. When the dog looked up at him, Zack arched a brow and squared his shoulders. Those big brown eyes weren't merry anymore. They were telling him to be smart and button up. Mrs. D had said he was protective.

As he took the dog back over to the fire to towel dry his rump, Zack reminded himself that normally when a member of the fairer sex started to push his buttons, he said goodbye. Easy. Cut off in a remote location by a freak snowstorm, not so easy this time.

But even if they weren't snowed in, he wouldn't walk away. Not yet. Because like it or not, Trinity had gotten under his skin in a way no one else had ever managed, and clearly he'd gotten under hers.

Six

A text on Zack's cell flashed five minutes after the power flickered back on around noon. Trinity studied his thoughtful expression as Zack read the message while she rocked the baby, who was drifting off for a postlunch nap.

"Cressida Cassidy from Child Services," he said. "Roads are still blocked. Tomorrow's the soonest they can get out. Still no word on leads about the baby's situation. The media hasn't gotten the story yet."

Trinity dropped a soft kiss on the baby's brow. Where had this little darling come from? It was as if she hadn't existed before she and Zack had happened upon her. Hard to believe that *no one* was out looking. That she wasn't missed. Trinity had always found comfort knowing that, for as long as she'd been able, her own mother had tried to find her.

But, whatever this baby's situation, for the time being at least, Bonnie was here, safe and warm. And if the price was sharing time with a man who stooped to any level to win and dominate, she'd see her way through.

She wouldn't mention what Kate had told her about his unscrupulous dealings with James Dirkins. It would only make her angry and she didn't want to raise her voice and upset the baby. She'd like to give him the benefit of the doubt but didn't Kate's latest gossip surrounding Zack fit? Making Dirkins feel responsible for his son's death for leverage... It made her sick to think about it.

Zack was glaring at the screen. "Wonder what the paparazzi will dig up and spin when they get a hold of the story."

Trinity bristled. *She* was part of the paparazzi. Or that's how he'd consider her, anyway.

"Tell Ms. Cassidy the baby's fine," Trinity managed to mumble. "I'll take care of her."

He frowned then slowly nodded.

Brows knitted and a pulse beating in his cheek, Zack texted back. He'd never complained about the baby, or her, being here. After his initial gripe, he hadn't said a word about Cruiser joining them, either; Zack had found his name on the tag buried beneath all that hair.

But she'd noticed Zack repeatedly catching the time on his wristwatch. He'd peer out those windows, rocking back on his heels, scanning the scene as if willing the sun to break through and the snow to melt clean away. He was edgy. Feeling crowded. These confined conditions were obviously a challenge. A drag.

For her own part...

Trinity tucked the wrap under Bonnie's chin.

Well, she was feeling remarkably comfortable—with the baby at least. Whenever Zack was close, it was exactly the opposite. Her endorphin levels surged over the bar to a point where she felt giddy. Earlier today she'd toyed with the idea that he might have felt something similar when he was around her. But with her blinkers off, Trinity could see that last night's kiss in front of the fire—this morning's suggestion of the time out at the Bahamas—had meant nothing more to Zack than an opportunity to slough off some sexual tension and try his luck. His competitive male brain was programmed that way.

And now they would be here together another night....

What would she do if he brought out the red wine and brandy and tried his charm on her again? Not that she wanted him to. But with the lights off and his magic switched on, the urges he brought out in her were difficult to deny. She could tell him she wasn't interested.

But what if he cut her off with a mind-robbing penetrating kiss? She might not approve of his character, but his seduction techniques were certainly a force. Was he the type who preferred sex fast and furious, or did he craft every move, absorb every touch…savor every sip? How would it feel to have Zack Harrison's hips grinding above hers, his mouth and tongue and teeth on her neck as she exploded and came apart in his arms?

Zack was at her side now, running a fingertip around the baby's cheek. "She looks like she might go down again."

Coming back to reality, Trinity scolded herself. *Concentrate. He asked about the baby.*

"I, eh, don't think she's ready yet."

"Why don't you sit for a while then?"

"She likes the movement." The rocking.

"Even if your arms fall off?"

She tested him. "Care to take over?"

He studied the baby but eventually his hand dropped away. "You're the expert."

"Not where wearing people down are concerned."

He looked at her sideways. "Do you want to explain that comment?"

"No." She took a breath. "Except to say if we're spending another night together, I'll be sleeping in one room and you'll be sleeping in another."

His smiling eyes dropped to her mouth. "I thought you liked camping out."

"What happened last night in front of the fire—" she walked back to the baby's recliner "—it won't happen again."

"No?"

Her back to him, she confirmed, "No."

"And if I decide to wear you down?"

His deep voice was at her ear, husky enough to send a wave of heat curling through her veins. In quick time, she tamped down the flame and turned to face him. But she hadn't banked on just how close he'd be, his broad chest so near, the rugged angles of his face slanting over hers. At this range, his presence was phenomenal...larger than life.

With his dark gaze penetrating hers, she fought to straighten her thoughts.

"I'm the enemy, remember? Aren't you afraid I'll get too close and expose all your secrets?"

His gaze turned hard then cold. "You're welcome to them."

When he moved away, Trinity felt the adrenaline drain from her body. The sooner this time was over, the better. She just prayed the authorities found Bonnie's mother soon.

He crossed to stoke the fire while she continued to sway with the baby. After a few more minutes, feeling confident Bonnie was about to nod off, Trinity eased the baby down onto the freshly laundered blanket on the recliner and bit by bit straightened.

When Bonnie shifted, Trinity thought she was merely getting comfortable. But then she moved again, blinked open her big blue eyes and, curious, Cruiser padded back from the fire to check. At the same time the baby gave a whimper, Trinity remembered her foster mother's favorite saying: *doesn't hurt to let them cry.*

And cry and cry and *cry.*

The short time Nora Earnshaw had looked after that baby so long ago was the best and worst time of Trinity's childhood. Only young herself, Trinity had helped where she could, eager to fetch a diaper or a rattle if the baby got tired of her singing and stories of white unicorns with golden horns and wings. But bedtimes were strict. When 7:00 p.m. arrived and teeth were brushed, Trinity wasn't allowed out of her room.

Maybe the baby cried because he'd wanted a bottle, but Trinity had always thought he'd simply wanted someone to sing to him. Lots of times she'd come close to taking the risk and sneaking out, but to her shame she never had. Instead she'd lain stiff while hot tears slid from the corners of her eyes and she'd stared, sick to her stomach, into the everlasting shadows. Into the dark.

Even now she wanted to cover her ears to the memories.

Back firmly in the present, Trinity swooped to pick Bonnie up again. If she was spoiling her, too bad. She'd rather a child have too much than too little. Who could ever say they had too many cuddles?

From the corner of her eye, Trinity saw Zack taking in the scene but he didn't offer an opinion. Slotting the poker away, he sauntered back to his laptop, which was open on the table, while she rocked the baby some more.

Twenty minutes later, when Bonnie finally looked completely gone and Trinity's back was ready to break, she carefully, carefully lay her down. But no sooner had her fingers slipped away than the baby pulled a face and shifted again. Her heavy eyelids dragged opened, her precious bottom lip began to quiver and Trinity's heart broke in two. What was she doing wrong?

She checked the baby's satin brow. No temperature. Collecting Bonnie again, she glanced around. Light snow was still filtering down outside but, to a degree, daylight brightened the room.

She asked Zack, "Can you draw some blinds?"

Rather than spend all day in pj's or change into business clothes, Zack had found her a pale blue cashmere sweater, which served wonderfully as a soft, comfy dress. He'd donned a sweater, too, dark slate in color to match his eyes. Coupled with a pair of well-loved jeans that hugged his buns and long athletic legs just right, he looked like every woman's *GQ* dream come to life. Well, he *was*.

Now those broad cashmere-covered shoulders squared as he stood tall, ready for action.

"Those windows don't have blinds."

None at all? "Don't you believe in privacy?"

"We're in the middle of nowhere. No one's going to peep unless it's a bear."

"I thought she might settle if it was dark. I'm going to try her in my room." The one where she kept her overnighter and changed Bonnie. "It'll be quieter in there, too." No rattling of coffee cups or Cruiser's claws clicking over the timber floor. They wouldn't have to tiptoe around, holding their breath. "Can you get some pillows together?"

"I'm on it." He strode ahead.

When she crept in the darkened room, he was retrieving extra pillows from a walk-in closet. Without her having to ask, to make it snug, he positioned the pillows in a rectangle on the bed then stuffed another quilt around the outside to keep the structure sound. Trinity lowered the baby and, checking inside the suit, made sure again her diaper was dry.

Seconds then minutes ticked by. The baby didn't move. Maybe it was the lack of light; perhaps she was simply worn-out, poor love. Trinity only knew she felt so happy and relieved when Bonnie stayed asleep; she was torn between laughing and collapsing. But it only took Zack to approach her—to come near—for her senses to begin to stir in that different, R-rated kind of way.

His rumbling voice was extra low. "Success."

She hugged herself. "Fingers crossed."

"How long do babies' lunchtime naps last?"

"Guess we're about to find out. Hopefully a couple of hours."

She gave Bonnie one last heartfelt look before she followed Zack out. When he moved to click shut the door, she automatically set a hand on his arm. Beneath the fine wool, that limb felt like a length of warm steel, so inviting to the touch, despite it all, she found it difficult to let go.

Schooling her expression, she stepped back.

"Leave the door open a crack. I want to hear if she cries."

A corner of his too-kissable mouth quirked up at one side at the same time he leaned an inch closer and her pulse began to thud.

"My guess," he whispered, "is you'll be going back to check every two minutes."

She sighed. He was right. "Maybe we could set up some remote control audio device like a baby monitor so I don't wear a track in your floor."

"We might already have a monitor. One that comes with his own batteries." Zack looked down.

Cruiser lay in front of the door, his head dropping onto crossed front paws, his tail as still as midnight. Only his eyes, and the soft folds on his brow, moved as he shared looks between them both. Trinity wanted to bend down and hug his neck.

"He wants to take the first watch."

"This dog has experience." Zack ruffled one floppy ear. "Before he gets too entrenched, maybe we ought to tell him this posting is strictly temporary."

Trinity hid her wince. It hurt to hear what she already knew. As far as she and Zack went, they were proverbial ships passing on a stormy Colorado night, and hopefully the baby and Cruiser would be reunited with people who cared about them. Soon they'd all be separated with no reason to meet again. Like her and that baby so many years ago.

Back in the main area a few minutes later, Zack was checking out the contents of his fridge.

"After those leftover steaks, the dog won't need anything for a while." Hands on knees, the fridge light casting shadows over the chiseled planes of his face, he glanced at her. "You hungry?"

They'd had cereal earlier and nibbled cookies throughout the morning. Exhaling until her lungs were completely empty, she eased down into a recliner.

"I'm more tired than anything. I might just spread out for a while."

"Get a proper rest. There are a couple of bedrooms upstairs."

Yes, she knew. One of them was *his*. Safer to stay here.

"This'll do fine." She grabbed a quilt. "Cruiser won't have to go far looking for me when the baby wakes."

"The baby can cope for a couple of minutes without you."

"Doesn't hurt to be close."

Really wouldn't hurt to grab a few winks, either.

She closed her eyes…let her muscles and tendons relax and float. While a series of snapshots and snippets of conversation from these past hours wound through her mind, she snuggled down more.

She might have been drifting when a strange sensation began to niggle and take hold. In a heartbeat she was hyperaware of a scent and muffled sound at the same time she felt something shift around her shoulder.

Her stomach jumped and eyes snapped open. Zack stood over her. His hand was on the quilt, lifting it higher.

"Your cover slipped." He finished tucking the edge in around the back of her neck before drawing away. "I thought you were asleep."

She exhaled a groan and stretched an arm high. "Trying to."

When he turned on his heel, Trinity fought the urge to call him back. She knew what he was. Knew that he used people to get what he required.

But not in this case. With no thought of personal gain, he'd offered his help with Bonnie, and while she didn't need to fall into his arms and pretend she was special to him, neither did she have to be rude. This was his house, after all.

She shifted up a little. "I'm really just resting. It feels good to lounge around but…"

Zack prodded. "It's great to lounge around, but what…?"

"It's weird," she confessed, "but after taking care of Bonnie for so long, now, without her right here with me, it almost feels like a part of me is missing."

"It's a motherly thing."

She had to grin. "How would you know?"

"My sister-in-law said something the same the first time their eldest had a sleepover. She said it felt like a limb was cut off."

Trinity considered that and nodded. Made sense. A child was such an integral part of her mother. Or she should be.

He glanced toward that downstairs bedroom. "Cruiser's still on duty."

She angled up. The dog was in the exact same position as they'd left him and now Zack was taking a seat at the foot of her chair.

With her huddled up and Zack resting back against a neighboring recliner, one arm balanced on a bent knee, she forced herself to accept his proximity and they watched the fire's sleepy flames dance and curl. Listening to the faint snap and occasional tumble of ash, inhaling the aroma of fresh coffee, knowing the snow was falling gentler now… She tried to put all the negatives out of her mind and focus on this perfect peaceful moment.

She was nowhere near ready for Zack's somber question when it came.

"Trinity, what happened to your parents?"

A terrible ice-cold then burning heat flooded her middle. He'd caught her off guard…. She didn't talk about the past. She'd worked to put it behind her where the pain or numbness belonged. But she and Zack would never meet again and, while he might be curious now, it was a sure bet he'd forget her and their conversations much sooner than she ever would.

And, after thinking about her foster years just now, she felt an odd niggling need to share.

"I'd like to believe my mother loved me," she finally said, "even though I wasn't a product of love. My foster mother told me when I should have been too young to know that my mother was raped."

Swinging around, Zack swore under his breath. "Please tell me that woman's child-minding days are over."

"I keep in touch with a couple of people where I grew up. They assure me that she's long since retired."

He rolled back one shoulder and a measure of the distaste dragging on his mouth eased. "Did you have other family?"

"Apparently my grandparents wanted my mother to give me up. She fought to keep me, but one night, not long after I was born, I was taken away. To this day I don't know how the legalities were handled—I think some forging must have gone on— but it seems my grandparents thought she'd get over it. That eventually my mother would get on with her life…or, rather, the life they'd prescribed for her. She didn't, or couldn't. My mother left her home and set out to find me."

Trinity always smiled when she remembered that part of her story, but never for long.

"With no money or support," she went on, "my mom ended up on the streets. I found that all out when I hired a P.I. a couple of years back. He also learned that my mother died a day before her twentieth birthday."

Zack's jaw was thrust forward but his eyes were glistening enough for Trinity to see her own reflection. "Your grandparents?"

"They've both passed away. As far as that P.I. could ascertain, they never tried to find me. My mother was an only child so there are no uncles or aunts, either."

He bowed his head, shook it once and murmured, "I'm sorry. I can understand why you made that decision."

"Which decision?"

"Not to have a family of your own. That's a lot to cope with. A lot to forgive."

Forgiveness was a strange concept, Trinity thought now, gazing into the fire. She'd heard a person needed to forgive a wrong committed against them in order to get on with their lives. But she'd gotten on with hers without needing to forgive. She could stem the tears. She could logically plan for the future. That's why she'd made that promise not to have children of her own and, since that time, had never second-guessed it. Had never thought differently.

Until today.

Taking care of Bonnie was so rewarding. Felt so worthwhile. Of course she didn't plan to run off and get pregnant or anything as crazy as that. But for the first time, she truly understood why, in times so full of uncertainty, people took the risk and brought innocent defenseless lives into this world.

Why people took a chance on falling in love.

Trinity had been asleep for an hour when Cruiser padded over to where Zack stood, hands slotted into the back pockets of his jeans, studying the vast panorama of snow. The dog knocked his nose against Zack's leg and gave a barely audible *gruff*. It took one-point-five seconds to interpret. Bonnie was stirring.

He wondered why Cruiser hadn't gone to Trinity instead. Most likely because the mistress was sound asleep while the master was whiling away the time, daydreaming about how different, peaceful—lonely?—the place would be tomorrow after the snow had started to melt and everyone had gone their respective ways.

Be that as it may, he was the "fetch it" guy. Trinity took care of the baby.

He could always steer Cruiser over to where she lay curled up on that recliner. But he'd used up that card this morning when the baby was wet and he'd cleared his throat hoping Trinity would wake and take the pressure off. Of course, that had been before he'd heard the rest of her story.

Good Lord. What an eye-opener. He'd known his life was

blessed a hundred different ways. A great family. A terrific childhood, even if his father hadn't been around half as much as he should. When Trinity had admitted her mother had been a victim of rape *then* had suffered such injustice at the hands of her own parents…

Zack grimaced.

Who in the name of God could scheme to get rid of their own blood? To his mind, a child conceived through such a violent act deserved consideration, protection, all the more. It was surreal to know that same child was the woman asleep on his lounge now.

He couldn't hope to grasp how she must feel. How she dealt with that past brewing in the back of her brain every day. Or perhaps she'd succeeded in blocking it out most of the time. Isn't that what survivors sometimes did?

Probably good those grandparents were deceased. Since Trinity's confession, he'd needed to tamp down the urge to form a plan to seek them out, and not to host a family reunion. His own Gran and Pap were the backbone of the Harrison clan. Where family was concerned, no sacrifice was too big for either one. Never having known that kind of bond, would Trinity feel alien in his family's company?

Although no family—including his—was without its hiccups. And shadows, past and present. They simply kept them better hidden than most.

Cruiser's snout nudged again and Zack came back to the situation at hand. *Baby awake. Captain needed on deck.* He blew out a breath and shook out his hands. He could do this. Hell, it was the *least* he could do.

Zack padded past Trinity's recliner. She was breathing evenly, brow smooth, eyes closed. His fingers itched to touch the silky sweep of her hair but he wouldn't risk waking her. This shift was his.

With another nose nudge, Cruiser knocked open the bedroom door. Zack pulled up his sleeves and inched inside. The baby was awake, watching her fingers wriggle in the shadows. Her gaze roamed, quickly found his and she kicked her legs in their wrap as if saying hello the only way she knew how.

Zack remembered how soaked she'd been that morning. But he was a man who commanded many and normally never backed off from a challenge. This couldn't be too hard. *Just get your mind around the problem, Harrison, and do it!*

In a fluid movement, he scooped her up and, holding her firmly, tested her padded behind with a palm.

Not wet. No leakages around the legs. He rolled back his shoulders. That was good enough for him.

He cradled her in one arm, waited for the inevitable—for her chin to dimple and bottom lip to drop. But she only gazed up at him, blowing bubbles and wriggling her toes in her leggings. Zack's throat clogged. *Sweetheart* was definitely the word.

Cruiser gave his leg a bump and Zack growled down. "Stop pushing already. I'm here, aren't I?"

He moved out to the main room, thinking about his next step. Bonnie had had a bottle before going to sleep. She shouldn't be hungry, but she did look wide-awake. He had experience with older kids. They were easy to entertain. But a three-month-old? No success. In fact, plenty of failures.

What was he supposed to do now?

Waking slowly, Trinity sucked in a breath then noticed that the light in Zack's living room where she'd fallen asleep had changed. From the shadows stretching over the timber floor, it was long past midday. More like midafternoon. However long she'd slept, she certainly felt refreshed. Bonnie must still be sleeping soundly, Trinity thought as she shifted to sit straighter in the recliner, or she'd have heard from Cruiser.

Enjoying a stretch and a yawn, she rubbed her eyes but stilled when she heard a sound rumbling nearby. Zack's voice. But there was another noise. A gurgling. *Giggling.*

On a burst of energy, Trinity scrambled up on her knees so that she could peer over the back of the recliner.

She couldn't believe her eyes.

This *had* to be a dream.

Propped up on forearms, Zack was lying on his front on a blanket on the floor. The baby was propped up on a bank of pillows opposite. Zack was shaking something that rattled and wobbled. Trinity had no idea what it was or how he'd come by it. She only knew the baby thought the sight and sound hilarious.

Zack was smiling, too, in a way that both surprised and warmed Trinity to her core. In that instant, in her mind, he was transformed. No longer simply the handsome, ruthless hotelier, but so much more a regular guy in sexy blue jeans who obviously enjoyed making a little girl laugh. Trinity wanted to laugh, too, even as moisture welled in her eyes. If she didn't disapprove of him so much, she might even be convinced to like him.

He glanced across and that glossy lock of hair fell over his brow as he beamed out a dazzling smile.

"Hey, look who's up."

"What's going on?" Trinity moved off the recliner, thinking how goofy her expression must be. She couldn't stop grinning and her voice was tellingly thick. "How long has she been awake?"

A sound came from behind Bonnie's bank of pillows. Cruiser's snout popped up, smiling and panting as usual. Zack shook the rattle again.

"We've been playing for around fifteen minutes."

"Is she wet?"

"She wasn't when she woke up. She's made me work since."

Trinity's palm caught her chest, and not totally to mock him. "You *changed* her?"

"I did. Fed her, too, when she started to grizzle."

Trinity made her way over. "So I've lost my job. Changing, feeding, maybe some rocking…"

"Whoa." Zack tipped onto to his side and she caught a long, horizontal view of "totally carefree and masculine" that would fit superbly in the center of a ladies' magazine. "Let's not get carried away."

He said the words but didn't look half as reticent as he had before and, across the way, the baby was throwing out her arms to him like she'd been doing it her whole life. Bonnie wanted the toy Zack held. Trinity was curious, too. Joining them, she sat cross-legged on the floor. That's when she saw the stash… a pile of similar-looking toys—colorful homemade stuff— bunched up by Zack's side.

"My nephews and nieces pass on these treasures all the time. We have dolls with wobbly heads." He shook the rattle then swapped it for a stuffed sock with pipe-cleaner whiskers. "As well as lots of animals. The teachers keep them busy in preschool."

From a distance, she eyed a duck, a giraffe and a horse with three legs and a trio of purple-button eyes to match. A brown plaster disc with odd markings left her stumped, though.

"What's that?"

He collected the piece. "Tom-Tom the Turtle."

When the baby stretched out her arms and wiggled her fingers, Trinity held her tiny hand in hers. "Oh, you can't have that, sweetie."

"There's nothing sharp. Nothing that'll fall off."

"She'll put it straight in her mouth."

Zack jumped up, rinsed the turtle under a steamy faucet, shook it off and brought him back. "All clean." He handed Tom-Tom over to a bedazzled Bonnie. "I'm sure Nicki won't mind."

"Who's Nicki?"

"My second-oldest nephew. This was last year's birthday gift."

"And that?" She nodded to a face with a fluffy yellow mane.

"Loger Lion. No body, I'm afraid. He was from Ava my niece for Christmas. She's four."

"Loger?"

"Ava has trouble with *r*'s."

Her heart warming all the more, Trinity accepted Loger when Zack handed him over. She'd known he had lots of extended family, and it made sense kids liked to make gifts of their craft bits and pieces, but, "Why do you have all this *here?*"

"They're at my apartment, too. Some at the office. My brothers have eight kids between them. Believe me, that's a lot of bead picture frames and finger paintings to go around."

His dark eyes were sparkling, with pride. With love. Here was a side Zack had never shown, particularly not to the press. He'd never let go and *shared* himself like this with her. Then again, she wasn't normally one to share, either.

He chose another animal from his stockpile. "I was about to have Necky Giraffe duel with Loger."

"Necky?"

"I don't choose the names, remember?"

"Why can't they dance instead?"

His brow wrinkled in a delectable frown. "Because they're both guys."

"Guys can dance."

"Only with beautiful women."

His dark eyes shone as a ghost of a different, mischievous smile hooked his mouth. It was all Trinity could do to keep from pushing common sense aside and doing something stupid like leaning forward to brush her lips over his. Instead she shelved the urge and concentrated on working out the show Necky and Loger were set to perform.

"Guys can dance together," she pointed out, "*if* you're a lion who's taken classes and wants to show his best friend how much he's improved. Loger used to have two left feet."

He grinned. "All these years and I never knew." He slid over to give her space on the blanket beside him. "Have a seat. There's plenty of room."

Trinity's heartbeat skipped. The urge to do precisely what

Zack suggested was so strong, the impulse was a little scary. But his mood was more light not seductive, and with Bonnie looking so happy and content…why not?

She shimmied over and lay down on her belly beside Zack and facing the baby. While Bonnie sucked on Tom-Tom, Trinity held up Loger. The baby sat riveted, waiting for the show.

Rolling a little toward Trinity to accommodate the movement, Zack trotted out his giraffe.

"My dear Mr. Loger," he began, but she interrupted.

"On second thought, maybe it should be *Miss* Loger." She was a girl, after all.

He set off again. "My dear *Miss* Loger, I couldn't help but notice how luminous your mane looks today."

"I did wash and straighten it very carefully."

She looked from the animals to Zack. He was smiling, not at the show or at Bonnie, but at her. An amused, highly appreciative look.

"Would you care to dance?" he finally asked.

She waited for her heart to stop beating in her throat before she replied, "But there's no music."

"I'll sing to you."

And this time, while the baby giggled and, engrossed, sucked Tom-Tom more, Trinity heard a different, deeper note in Zack's voice. Her skin started to heat and thoughts began to veer to places best kept under lock and key.

"I don't think that's a good idea."

But he tipped closer and insisted. "I'll sing about your eyes."

Trinity quivered to her curling toes. He'd spoken near her ear and she knew without looking that his gaze was intent, on her profile…on her lips. She tried to get her suddenly whirling thoughts back on track.

"Maybe we should find a song we already know."

"Know what I really want to sing about?" His warm breath brushed her hair. "How much I enjoyed holding you last night."

A series of brush fires ignited and raced through her blood.

She ought to move away. Tell him to stop. With him so near, devouring her with that hungry gaze, she wanted to forget what she knew and admit that she'd enjoyed it, too.

When his mouth grazed her temple, she tingled and weakened more. "Dance with me, Trin," he murmured. "Dance with me tonight."

As his chin grazed a lazy path around her cheek and his fingers slid away from the giraffe, a spike of adrenaline shot through her and finding her senses, dropping the lion, she leaned away. Got to her feet. Unbalanced, flushed, she pushed back hair fallen over her brow.

"I should probably get a bottle ready for Bonnie."

He gazed up at her, his dark gaze intense. Determined. "I already fed her, Trin. She's perfectly happy."

"Then I'll put on coffee."

"I don't want coffee. I want you."

He reached for her but she dodged his touch and, panicked, crossed to the kitchen. Her body burning, she felt his gaze on her while she collected the pot with a trembling hand. Would he follow her? Run his hot palms over her shoulders, down her sides? God help her, she wanted that. Wanted him. And she shouldn't.

Couldn't.

She was a convenience, nothing more, no matter how wanted he made her feel.

When he began to talk again to the baby while she saw to the coffee, Trinity let out a long breath, but the craving didn't ease. She closed her eyes and imagined him kissing her objections away, almost felt his mouth sliding over her body and his hard, long length bearing down. Despite the absurdity of it all, she wanted those things badly.

In fact, she was beginning to want this—the whole package—way too much.

Seven

Zack growled. "Cruiser, get your nose out of there."

"He's definitely found something," Trinity said.

Probably scaring the life out of some poor squirrel, Zack thought.

Cruiser barked. Propped up in Trinity's arms, Bonnie screeched and, delighted, tried to clap her hands.

After the Loger/Necky scene, the mood had been strained. When the sun had poked through its thinning cover of clouds and the snow looked as if it was covered with a billion scattered diamonds, Zack had suggested they all get some fresh air. He'd loaned Trinity some boots that were way too big and an overcoat that came down past her shins. After bundling the baby in blankets, he'd shrugged into a bomber jacket and had led the other three outside.

He hadn't intended the toy pantomime to veer off in that direction, with his instincts taking over and body leading where he clearly wanted to go. And Trinity's determination to refuse him only made the need stronger. More insistent. Watching her saunter around in his cashmere sweater all morning had driven him near crazy. At one point, when the baby had been down, he'd very nearly crowded her into a corner and spoken to her in a language she *had* to understand. Could be something to do with deprivation of sensation—being stuck out here on their own—but whenever she was remotely near, every cell in his nervous system lit up like a pinball machine and gravitated toward her. And he could see in her eyes, hear in her voice, she felt it, too.

Tomorrow Child Services would be out and that would be the end of playing house. But before they said goodbye, he was determined to have Trinity curled up around him, murmuring his name while they made love throughout the night. He needed to end the anticipation. Once and for all, put those fires out. But all that would need to wait till dark.

Now he packed a snowball in his hands and pitched a slider at Cruiser's butt. The dog jumped then crouched low before zipping off full speed at them, skidding out at the last minute and spraying snow all over them. Trinity was laughing while she checked the baby whose smile split her little face. When Zack pegged another, it hit Cruiser's leg and he did the galloping skidding thing all over again. But this time rather than running off, he arced around and caught the back of Zack's coat in his teeth and tugged, trying to drag him back.

"Hey, quit that!" Zack pulled the other way while Trinity and the baby ended up in fits.

When his jacket was finally free, he lunged at the dog who dodged at the last minute. Zack landed face-first in the snow.

His head shooting up, he blew snow from his mouth and caught Trinity's stage whisper to her conspirators.

"Quick, let's get him. Let's get Zack."

Cruiser was barking, his tail wagging furiously and the baby was squeaking, her arms going crazy while she giggled. Trinity pounced up and kicked snow over his back and legs at the same time the dog leaped over him, back and forth like a not-so-graceful steed in a steeple race.

Sliding in the mush, Zack got to his feet. He was outnumbered and cold and near out of breath from laughing. But he was far from defeated. Meaning business now, he prowled toward Trinity and Bonnie. Her eyes flashing in a stream of late afternoon sunshine, Trinity blinked several times then backed up toward the house.

"Okay. Game's over."

"Uh-uh. I don't think so."

"I'm holding the baby."

"She's in trouble, too." Cruiser barked and Zack narrowed his eyes at him. "Don't worry. You're next."

Zack belted forward and swung Bonnie out of Trinity's arms. After twirling her carefully in the air, he set her in her carrier, which sat in its upright position on the porch, then set off after Trinity. When he caught her, they both fell into the snow while Cruiser yapped and their laughter echoed through the trees. Then the dog trotted off to look out for the baby and suddenly everything other than a pair of beautiful violet-colored eyes faded into the background. His blood was singing, his senses sparking and she was trapped in his arms, her lips so pink and close and tempting. There was no escape. He was going to kiss her, and when he was finished, he'd take a breath and damn well kiss her again.

His gloved palm holding steady the back of her head, he slanted his head over hers. Because she was panting and winding down from a fit of laughter, he didn't have to work to part her lips. He struck gold on contact and, without thinking, she accepted then embraced his kiss.

As their tongues wound around each other and the sizzle morphed into a burn, he drew her shoulders in and gave her no room for doubt. He'd found the magic combination to her lock and now that she was open to the possibilities he wouldn't let anything hold them back.

Except, of course, the fact they had a three-month-old probably wondering why all her fun had stopped.

Reluctantly Zack forced his saner self to surface and broke the kiss, but his lips stayed close to hers. He meant for her to see the hunger blazing in his eyes.

"It's been a good afternoon," he murmured while his blood throbbed and, giving in, his head angled down again.

But, still out of breath, Trinity turned away. "We have to go in. Bonnie needs her bath."

"She's already had her bath."

"It's getting dark."

Grazing his lips over her cheek, he smiled. "I know."

"The baby—"

"Will sleep in the bedroom tonight and before you remind me about our responsibilities, it's a well-known fact that adults make love with babies in the house." His smile brushed her cheek.

She seemed to hold her breath. "It's not a good idea."

"It's possibly the best idea I've ever had."

"I don't even like you."

He frowned. "You don't know me."

"All the more reason—"

"For you to say yes…"

An hour later, Trinity emerged from that bedroom and announced, "She's down."

From the kitchen, Zack looked over. "That was easy. Is Cruiser at his post?"

"Couldn't drag him away if we tried."

"Ready to eat? We have omelet à la Zackery. Secret ingredients are mushrooms and cheese."

"Sounds delicious."

Trinity held the plates while he cut the omelet with his spatula, served up half each and, as usual, her nerve endings began to buzz. How would she ever survive the evening without having Bonnie as an excuse to put between herself, Zack and his confessed intent to finish what they'd begun last night and this afternoon in the snow.

Sitting at the table, he poured them both a generous glass of white wine then put some salad from a center bowl on his plate. While Trinity absently found some lettuce, Zack enthusiastically sliced into his eggs. She was moving a mushroom around when, on his second mouthful, he frowned.

"No good?"

"I'm sure it's delicious. I want to clear the air first."

He chewed, swallowed. "Clear away."

"About that kiss this afternoon."

"I'm sure our communication there couldn't have been clearer." His fork bobbed at her plate. "Your omelet's getting cold."

"But I'm not finished—"

"And if the baby wakes up you'll need some nourishment, so eat now. I promise I'll listen to everything you have to say later."

Trinity nibbled her lip. She didn't like the gleam in his eyes. She didn't think he'd give her any more of a chance to talk when they'd finished here. In fact, she could envisage him quietening her words with another of those devastating kisses. She had her ethics, but how could she hope to win against that?

But in a way he was right. Hopefully Bonnie was down for good, but bedtime and babies wasn't a science. And this omelet did smell and look divine. A growl from her stomach decided for her.

A few minutes later, halfway finished, she said, "This is really very good."

"I don't cook much. Back home I usually don't get out of the office until late. If we don't get food delivered and I don't have a dinner engagement, I pop into a great steak place a couple of blocks away."

"I'm amazed you don't have a bevy of women lining up to cook for you."

He sent her a knowing glance before collecting his wine goblet. "My brothers are the domesticated ones, remember."

She feigned an enlightened look. "How did I forget?"

They both knew women lined up to do a whole lot more than flip Zack's steak. Although…

"The way you were getting along with Bonnie this afternoon, anyone might be fooled into thinking you're a regular family man."

That he might actually enjoy having his own wife and child around. Which was crazy. Zack was a bachelor businessman, pure and simple.

Although hadn't she had a change of heart since caring for Bonnie? Yesterday a seed had been replanted, and now she couldn't deny feeding into the fantasy of having a child of her own. Having a husband, a family…

Oh, but she was getting all muddled when, tonight like never before, she needed to keep everything straight.

Zack's brows dipped before he drained the wine from his glass and made a sound of deep satisfaction in his throat. "This really is an exceptional year."

Having tasted the wine, she had to agree. But no matter how enjoyable, she didn't intend to indulge beyond one glass tonight. After that incredible kiss in the snow, he'd told her exactly how he felt. He wanted to make love to her. Sitting across from Zack now, looking so casual yet dynamic, if she was a weaker woman, she might easily fling her napkin to one side and suggest they cut dinner short.

But as much as she'd enjoyed the day and having the opportunity to see this other more human side of Zack, those other darker considerations kept weighing on her mind. She'd known he liked women, that he was beyond ruthless in business, but to discover via Kate this morning that he'd used another man's sorrow to move closer to a contract's finish line? It set her teeth on edge.

She was attracted to Zack in a way she hadn't known existed

but she couldn't live with herself if she put physical need before her conscience. Not that iron man Zack would understand that.

When his cell lying on the counter buzzed, Zack went to check the message. Without replying to the text, he returned to the table and drew his chair in.

He took a long pull from his glass and explained, "Dirkins wants to see me tomorrow."

Trinity sat straighter. "Do you think he's ready to meet your offer?"

Had he succeeded in wearing the poor man down?

Zack collected his fork again. "Yes, I think he's ready to sign."

"Guess you finally got to him."

He studied her then shrugged. "I'm sorry. You've lost me."

Should she tell him what she knew or should she accept that she could do nothing to change the way Zack approached life and let it slide? The only rule in *his* world was "there are no rules." Even when it came to an anguished father's emotions. A broken man who'd been knocked down twice—once by the death of his son and again when Zack had insinuated he was in some way to blame.

Trinity shifted her plate away. Right or wrong, she needed to know. "How did James Dirkins's son die?"

"Car accident." Zack patted his mouth with his napkin and thoughtfully set it back down on his lap. "Some say it was suicide. Apparently he'd been troubled of late."

"Apparently? So you did some research?"

His gaze sharpened. "Where's this going?"

She couldn't keep quiet. She had to ask, and if Zack didn't want to admit that he'd played on this man's feelings to gain an upper hand, she wouldn't be surprised. Men like Zack rarely took responsibility. They only plundered the rewards. Or that's the way the media depicted him.

But the man she'd come to know a little came across as more complex than that, and certainly capable of compassion. Being part of his pantomime for Bonnie and those games when they'd fooled around in the snow… Could that story about Zack putting those kinds of emotional screws into Dirkins really be true?

"When I spoke to Kate this morning," Trinity began, "she said you'd let Dirkins know you believed he was somehow responsible for his son's death."

Zack's brow furrowed and his gaze darkened until the irises appeared black. His voice was low and grating. "She said *what?*"

Her cheeks flushing, Trinity pushed back her chair. "I shouldn't have said anything."

"'You' being Trinity Matthews or the so-called free press?" He swore and dropped his fork on his plate before he met her gaze again. "Usually it doesn't bother me, living in a society where everyone is consumed by what the other half wear and eat and say. It's a circus. Three parts illusion and the other part bullshit."

Trinity's heartbeat was crashing high in her chest. She hadn't expected this reaction. Was this some kind of show to get her on his side? Gain her sympathy? Or was he better than the press made out? Than even Zack might sometimes give himself credit for?

"Are you saying you didn't suggest to James Dirkins that he as good as killed his own son?" she asked.

"Does it matter what I say? You people print what sells." His lip curled. "And you think *I* should be ashamed of myself."

His expression, his tone, the conviction of his words…

She gave a hapless shrug and muttered, "I didn't say it was true."

He looked at her hard then huffed like he was tired of it all. His plate in hand, he moved to the kitchen.

She glared at her own plate then came up with an idea that might work for everyone.

"Even if Dirkins can't manage it on his own anymore, he must be torn. It'd feel like he was saying goodbye to his son again. Maybe there's some other option where he can still be a part of the hotel without having to take all the responsibility. What if you offered him a partnership?"

His dish rattled into the sink. "I don't do partnerships."

Her lips and stomach tightened. "Of course you don't." How could she forget? His brothers believed in partnerships, not Zack.

He moved back to the table. "I'm not a bad guy. I go out of my way to be fair in business, to be a good son and uncle." He reached, found her hand and pulled her to her feet. "And in case you hadn't noticed, I'm also a man who has normal desires and needs."

She caught her breath but, defiant, challenged his gaze. "I'd noticed."

"Tomorrow the authorities will come and take that baby away. Hopefully they'll find her parents but either way our involvement will end." His fingers brushed down her forearm, gripped her hand. "That doesn't mean we have to stop seeing each other."

The world tilted beneath her feet. Everything was suddenly way out of balance.

"You want to see me again?"

He brought her close. "What do you think?"

His mouth dropped over hers and her body flashed with an energy that had been building all day, that had bubbled on the brink of boiling over since she'd put the baby down. Now the fuel racing through her blood rushed to her core, making her feel heavy and hot and desperate for him to make good on the promise he'd made today. The promise about making love.

His hand cupped her cheek, directing the slant of her head while he worked a kiss that left her floating inches off the floor. The sensations and emotions were so powerful she wanted to thread her arms around his neck and forget about what was wrong or right, or smart or pathetically stupid. She was smoldering, unable to pretend she could walk away before experiencing more. And wasn't that only human? Why shouldn't she have this night? There was nothing stopping them except her pride. If this was a mistake, she'd need to live with it, like everything else.

She'd all but surrendered, fanning her palms up over Zack's hard cashmere-covered chest, when his caress changed in tempo and in tone. His kiss was still expert and breathtakingly thorough but in her heart she was aware he knew he'd won. And as his hand moved higher and his fingers splayed up through her hair, she was at a loss to do anything other than sigh in surrender and dissolve that much more. The hard length of his body seemed to combine so seamlessly with hers, she couldn't think where he finished and she began.

With his mouth still on hers, he swept her up into his arms. A moment later, she was vaguely aware of passing by Cruiser. Before he started up the stairs, his chest expanded on a breath and he reluctantly dragged his mouth from hers. As he peered down through lidded eyes, feeling the hammer of his heartbeat pumping through her own blood, she fought to get her breath.

"I can walk up myself," she offered, "if I'm too heavy."

The white of his teeth shone in the shadows as he flashed a smile. "I'll manage."

He carried her up to the second floor while Trinity's pulse throbbed and her grasp of reality seemed to fall away. As he crossed to the center of a room draped in quiet shadows, she recalled her first impression of him in the cab, how his presence had dominated and his deep voice had more than intrigued. Later she'd thought how attractive his lips were, particularly the fuller lower one. She'd wondered how their bows would feel grazing over hers, never dreaming for a moment she'd find out.

Now as he stopped before the foot of a king-size bed, the need to know Zack Harrison intimately and all night was so powerful, she positively *ached* with it. After vowing never to succumb, at this high-octane moment she was leagues beyond ready.

First moving to elbow on a corner light, he then angled to flick back the covers before laying her gently on the bed. One knee on the mattress, the other foot on the floor, he sculpted a slow teasing hand over her shoulder while running a band of barely there kisses over every erogenous point from her brow to the sweater's V at her breasts.

But in a corner of her mind an image of the baby, alone in that bedroom downstairs, sneaked in and, dragging herself from the headiness, Trinity sat up.

"What if Bonnie wakes and we don't hear?"

His focus shifted to lifting the sweater up over her hips, her waist.

"I can attest to the fact," he said, "that she'll only have to squeak before Cruiser bounds up here to let us know."

Her arms came up, the sweater came off and his heavenly mouth came down again, this time to taste a bone-melting trail along the sweep of one shoulder at the same time he snapped the clasp at her back. As the bra fell, those tantalizingly mouth-on-skin drops angled lower until he was lightly sucking the tip of one breast and she was going out of her mind. When the stiff tip of his tongue twirled a slow wet circle then flicked a few mind-blowing times, the buildup of sensations overflowed their dam.

While his palms on her bare back pressed her closer, she let her neck roll to one side and plied her fingers through his hair. When his head came away and cool air hit hot flesh, he urged her back down onto the sheet before drawing that other nipple deeply into his mouth.

Her mind floating and body humming, she soaked up the pleasure and waited. She imagined his tongue soon trailing lower as his slightly roughed fingertips grazed over tender peaks, rolling and gently pinching the tips. Instead his mouth drew completely away a moment before the furnace of his body left her, too. Bringing her arms up around to circle her head, she frowned and forced open her eyes.

He stood at the side of the bed, catching the back of his

sweater then dragging the wool forward over his head before dropping it at his feet. With his hair mussed and his magnificent body backlit, a silver halo shone out from around his broad shoulders' expanse. So muscular and bronzed, she couldn't take her eyes off the extraordinary figure he cut.

He flicked open the button on his jeans, eased the zipper down and when he pushed on the hips, the denim rustled to the floor. In the shadows, she could make out the line of dark hair that arrowed from his navel to black briefs that were having a hard time keeping his erection penned in.

When he came to her, the light changed and every working muscle was cast in a mesmerizing show of rippling relief. He stopped to hover mere inches above her. Adoring his musky scent, she filled her lungs and threaded her arms around his neck.

"I've thought about this moment," he said, "from the second you slipped into my cab."

"From the very first second?" she teased.

He grazed his beard over her cheek. "Hmm…maybe before."

She drove her hands up over the muscled contours of his shoulders, relishing the anticipation, and whispered close to his ear.

"Then we shouldn't waste any more time."

His hand trailed up her leg then detoured to find that most sensitive part of her. While he dropped soft, slow kisses down her neck, across her shoulder, two fingertips trailed up her center then settled into circling that swollen burning bead.

Everything but sensation dropped away. She was only aware of the slow, delicious flame that she never wanted to go out as his circling touch slowed to an agonizing pace that felt so incredible, she had to bite her lip and hold onto his arm to stop from grinding against him. But then he shifted, and she was left trembling on the edge.

Next thing she knew, he was easing inside her, his mouth covered hers and his hand found its way between them again.

Trinity snatched back a breath as a bolt of heat ripped through her core. She was so close, she could see the orgasm in her mind, calling her nearer...hotter...higher.

When the friction between them reached fever pitch, he thrust in a final time and her world imploded with wave after wave of incomparable pleasure. She rode a roll of continuous peaks, murmuring his name, clinging to his heat, thanking fate.

And cursing it, too.

Eight

"I'm glad you talked me into that."

Agreeing wholeheartedly, Zack flipped Trinity over and on top of him then wove his palms over the satiny plane of her back, down over the smooth rise of her behind.

"You really didn't need much persuading."

"Must be the isolation."

He grinned. "Cabin fever?"

"I'm still a little restless."

His hands curved in and went deeper. "Good, because I'm nowhere near finished with my remedy."

Her smile slid over to capture his mouth. It seemed they hadn't stopped kissing and yet he couldn't imagine ever growing tired of the way her tongue danced with his—sometimes darting and hungry. At other times, like now, sensual, weaving...coaxing blood to rush to places that were more than ready for Act II. He'd never felt so satisfied and yet so ready for more.

He was repositioning her hips over his, seriously considering grabbing another condom and taking this joining to the next heart-pumping level, when a little of her kiss's enthusiasm seemed to wane. Zack craned his neck, deepened the kiss but gradually her lips left his. In the misty light, he frowned up as she peered with a guilty look glistening in those beautiful thickly lashed eyes.

"Are you tired?" he asked.

"A little uneasy."

Grinning, he swept her over until he was the one on top. "I know how to fix uneasy."

He lowered his mouth to her throat and began to work his way inch by delectable inch down. But rather than feel her sink into the mattress and melt beneath him, she held back. Stiffened. His head came up and he frowned.

"Am I losing my flair?"

She caught him under the arms and he let her drag him up. She looked so concerned, his chest squeezed. Whatever her worry was, he wanted to kiss it all away.

"Would it be silly," she asked, "to move back downstairs?"

"You want to be nearer the baby?"

"I know Cruiser's there on watch," she went on. "I know she probably won't wake until morning." She fingered a lock of hair away from his eyes. "Just somehow I'd feel better."

He thought it through and nodded. "Me, too."

Her face split with a smile. "Really?"

"On one condition. We stay warm only through body heat and the fire. As sexy as I find them, I don't want a hint of red silk pj's coming between us tonight."

She snatched a happy kiss and stayed close to rub the tip of his nose with hers. "Deal."

While she visited the bathroom, he found two oversize robes from his walk-in closet and slipped a couple of extra condoms in the largest robe's pocket. A moment later, they were "dressed" and stepping over Cruiser to pop their heads inside that downstairs bedroom.

A sidelight cast a soft glow over the room. Bonnie was sound asleep, her arms at right angles along either side of her head. Cruiser appeared to be off in doggy slumberland, too, although Zack wondered whether he was playing possum in case, for some reason, they tried to get him to move.

A moment later, while Trinity got herself snug under the quilts, Zack stoked the fire. When the flames were beyond toasty, he shirked out of his robe and joined her. He pulled at her sash and Trinity didn't object. She merely sat up, peeled the heavy sleeves off her shoulders and happily snuggled down against him, naked among the pillows and quilts.

Seeing her body briefly in the flickering of the fire glow only fed his intentions to make love again. And again. But she seemed so comfortable nestling against his chest, her cheek resting on one pec, her breath warm on his throat; he didn't want to disturb her. So he wound that arm more securely around her and dropped a lingering kiss on her sweet-smelling crown.

This day couldn't have had a better ending.

After the way Zack had brought her to climax, Trinity was content to simply lie here and reflect. But when her trailing nails brushed his growing erection, she couldn't help from turning her face to graze his flat nipple with her teeth while her hand clutched his shaft and dragged the length up to its tip.

His body locked at the same time his penis throbbed and he rubbed his lips over her hair.

"I was thinking you might want a break but I'm more than happy to play."

"We can talk as well."

He shuddered out a sigh. "Keep doing that and I'll agree to anything."

"What if I do this?"

She dragged her hand back and forth at the same time dabbing moist kisses between his sternum and his navel.

"I need to warn you right now how good that feels."

Teasing, she tugged again and his hips came off the floor.

"Tell me more about this house." *Your home.*

His eyes closed, he groaned and his head went to one side. "What do you want to know?"

"What drew you to it first?"

"It feels…peaceful." Her hand slid away and he growled. "You don't have to stop."

"I'm afraid you won't be able to carry on a conversation."

"Some say talk is overrated."

She rolled over more toward him and rested her chin on her bunched hand. "A sense of peace, you say."

"This whole town has it," he croaked. "At Christmas time, they put on a big evening of music and games for the kids. At the end of the night, a huge tree in the middle of Main Street gets lit up. The star at the top is massive."

"Sounds like a great place to raise a family," she said, half to herself.

"The family I bought this home from had twin boys. The dad would take them fly-fishing and hiking. Both times I came to look the house over, the entire place smelled of brownies baking. I like brownies."

"Ever tried to bake them yourself?"

"I usually pick some up from a shop in town." In the flickering light, his gaze sharpened. "Do you bake?"

"I used to do all the cooking when I was younger so now I avoid it every chance I get."

"Ever go hiking?"

"Never in Colorado."

He tucked one hand behind his head. While he smiled at some imaginary point beyond the ceiling, Trinity drank in the magnificent view of one bulging bicep.

"The scenery here is pretty amazing," he said. "The air when you really get out is the purest you'll ever breathe."

"Doesn't sound like you're in a hurry to get back to New York."

"New York's home."

"It doesn't have to be. Isn't the saying—'home is where the heart is'?"

He shifted so that she moved and he lay on his side facing her. As shadows danced over his arm, he curled hair back from her cheek and asked, "Where's your heart?"

The question took her aback. She thought and decided, "I guess I'm still searching."

"So not in writing for magazines?"

"That's what I do, Zack. Not who I am."

"Why can I see you working with children somehow?"

"I thought about it once. Believe it or not, I wanted to work somewhere in Child Services. But I didn't know if I was strong enough." She had a flashback to that much earlier darker time and winced. "Too close to it all, I guess."

"I think being close is exactly what a job like that needs. Any department or organization to do with children would be lucky to have you."

She wanted to hug him for that but… "I wouldn't feel as if I could ever do enough."

His grin was soft, encouraging. "Says you who obviously has so much to give."

When his gaze lowered to her lips and his mouth found hers again, Trinity was taken over by a wave of new emotions, feelings that left her so energized and at the same time strangely serene. Zack Harrison barely knew her, and yet this minute it felt as if he knew her better than anyone, including herself.

Nine

He was dreaming of a snarling tiger with foot-long canines pouncing on Bonnie, meaning to drag her away, when the rhythmic pounding of those distant jungle drums suddenly changed tack into a more conscious stream and Zack was thrown awake with a jolt.

Jumping up, Zack's reflexes sent his every sense flying to the source of the noise—the windows. One horrifying moment later, he realized what he was hearing and why. On the same breath, he understood that he was crouched in a defense/attack stance and wearing exactly no clothes.

He couldn't recall the last time he'd been embarrassed but he was darn sure he'd never forget this moment.

Ripping a quilt off the nearest recliner, he lashed the bulk as best he could around his hips at the same time Trinity groaned and, scratching her head, sat up. Wild hair. Big yawn. And no clothes there, either. Not a stitch.

Blinking drowsy eyes, she squinted up at him and frowned. "What's going on?"

"Someone's outside?"

"Someone else needing a home?"

"I'm pretty sure it's the woman from Child Services."

Trinity's questioning look turned to a mask of stark horror. And as her focus flew to the windows—to the woman wearing rubber boots and a dour face—he read Trinity's mind. Why had that woman come around the back? For Pete's sake, hadn't anyone heard of a front door?

While Trinity scooped her arms through a nearby robe and knotted the tie at her waist, Zack took a breath and crossed to open the door. Her boots were muddy but he wouldn't ask this visitor to come in via the mudroom entry.

She stepped inside with a, "Mr. Harrison. I'm Cressida Cassidy. I've caught you at a bad time."

"Not a bad time." He tossed an innocent look Trinity's way. "Would you say 'bad'?"

She shrugged and hugged herself in a robe that puddled around her feet. "Maybe a little inconvenient."

Ms. Cassidy's smile was paper-thin. "You didn't mention you were married."

"I'm not."

The woman blinked then sniffed. "I see."

He pushed on. "This is Trinity…" His mind went blank. "Ah, Trinity…"

Trinity threw out a welcoming hand. *"Matthews."*

Zack ran a hand through his bed hair. "Early mornings my brain doesn't work so well."

"It's after nine," Ms. Cassidy said, releasing Trinity's hand as if it might be contaminated with some rare STD. "I apologize for taking you both unawares. You may not know but a large trunk has fallen directly across the entrance to your front door. Rather than trying to scale the—"

A far-off cry interrupted Ms. Cassidy's tale. She blanched at the same time Zack froze and Trinity leaped off and into action. The baby sounded as if she'd been stuck with a pin.

While his pulse thudded in his temples, Zack forced himself to stand calmly as a clearly concerned Ms. Cassidy waited for Trinity's return.

As worry turned to suspicion, Ms. Cassidy's face began to harden and her double chin pulled in. "Mr. Harrison, where have you got that baby?"

An appeasing gesture, both Zack's palms went up. "She's perfectly safe. Cruiser's looking out for her."

"Who's Cruiser?"

At that moment, the dog barreled out and plowed into the backs of his legs. Zack winced and introduced the other member of the household. "Cruiser, Ms. Cassidy."

"You let a dog babysit?"

"Only last night. We were right here pretty much the whole time."

Her attention skated over to the empty wine bottle and her lips pursed. "I'd like to see the baby."

Trinity sang out. "Be there in a sec!"

While Ms. Cassidy tapped her boot, sending mud splatters over the timber floor, Zack zipped into the laundry room and pulled on some jeans and a T-shirt. He came out running a smoothing hand through his hair and wishing that Cruiser hadn't taken his babysitting job quite so seriously and had left his post long enough to warn them ahead of time about visitors. He and Trinity might not have heard a car arrive, but a dog's hypersensitive hearing must have.

"Trin must be changing her," Zack told Ms. Cassidy. "She wakes up soaked."

The woman's lips tightened more. After another brittle minute, she shifted to force her way past. Thank God Trinity was on her way back out. She was dressed in the business clothes she'd worn the day they'd met, although the skirt was crooked and some of her blouse buttons weren't fastened. The baby in her arms, however, looked happy and healthy and wide-awake.

"Have you found out anything?" Trinity asked their visitor as she stopped at Zack's side.

"We've located the mother," Ms. Cassidy said. "She's outside in a police car now."

Zack's blood pressure dropped. Police? "So something *is* wrong?"

"I'm not at liberty to say." Ms. Cassidy put out her arms. "I'll take her now."

Trinity turned a notch away; a natural enough reaction, Zack thought, feeling a twitch himself. If a person looked after a baby the way she had, of course they'd be shielding. Obviously they'd have grown attached.

"She'll need a bottle," Trinity said.

Ms. Cassidy replied, "The mother says she takes the breast as well as formula."

While Trinity stood agape, clearly lost for words, Zack stepped up. They had a right to know…didn't they?

"I think you can imagine how worried we've been for this little girl. How did she come to be in that cab all alone?"

"You'll appreciate, Mr. Harrison, there are legal issues regarding privacy involved here." Ms. Cassidy found an understanding smile. "But I assure you the mother is ecstatic to have her baby back. It was all an unfortunate mistake."

"Mistake?" he said. "I'm sorry, but that's hard to believe."

"I'll pass on your contact details," Ms. Cassidy said firmly, "and she can get in touch with you, if that's what she wants to do."

Zack's back teeth ground down. He burned to say more, for himself and Trinity, too, because as much as there was no way out, clearly she didn't want to hand the baby over like this. He felt the same way. Sure, Bonnie wasn't theirs. He supported privacy issues; he had people enough try to delve into *his* business and dig up the dirt. But didn't he and Trinity deserve at least an explanation?

Was the mother negligent? Did she have support? What's to say Bonnie wouldn't end up in a worse situation and soon?

The woman's arms were still out. Trinity took two deep breaths and then, her eyes glistening, carefully handed the baby over.

Cressida pulled back Bonnie's wrap to inspect her rosy cheeks and for the first time released a genuine smile. She glanced up. "Thank you, Mr. Harrison, Ms. Matthews, for looking after her."

Zack had fetched the car seat. With his other arm around Trinity's waist, he said, "We'll walk you out."

Not an offer. Rather a statement.

Together he and Trinity followed Ms. Cassidy and the baby back out the opened glass door and all four—five including Cruiser—set off along the snow-covered path.

The sun was out, uncommonly bright and warm, Zack thought. All around, snow was turning to slush and the air had that freshly washed smell he usually liked. As they rounded the path, two cars came into view in the driveway. In the backseat of the police car, a young woman sat holding her brow. Through the window, she looked decidedly wan.

As Zack grudgingly handed the carrier to Ms. Cassidy, his stomach muscles gripped and every hair on the back of his neck lifted. Surely they wouldn't hand Bonnie back if the mother was ill. Hell, maybe she was on drugs and didn't even remember leaving her baby in that cab.

Ms. Cassidy crossed to the police vehicle and while the policeman fit the carrier on the far passenger side, the baby was handed to the woman—*girl*—in the backseat. He heard her gasp and saw her snuggle Bonnie close. He should have felt relief. He only felt chilled. What was her story? Was there any way of finding out where she lived? He wouldn't sleep tonight. Maybe ever again.

Trinity was shivering beside him, more due to shock than the weather, he suspected.

"She looks sixteen," she murmured, "seventeen, tops."

Zack held her more firmly against him, her side to his. "Only a kid herself."

"She must have parents who can help."

"So where were they when the baby was left alone in that cab?"

Truth was they might never know.

Trinity curled into him more as they watched the young mother slide Bonnie into the car seat and buckled it up. When she sniffed, he almost felt her tears needing to break. Damn it, his throat was so clogged, he felt like crying himself.

Ms. Cassidy slid into her dark blue sedan and the policeman got into his vehicle while Zack stood there, feeling more helpless than he had in his life. He had this absurd urge to bolt over and snatch the baby back. He had to keep reminding himself…

She isn't ours, she isn't ours.

The police car was pulling out, Trinity's fingers were wound up in his T-shirt's front and Zack's heart had fallen to his knees. But when the car reached the end of the driveway, the wheels stopped turning, the back door swung open and the girl—the mother—came striding out.

She wore fashionably distressed blue jeans and a pink sweater. As she neared, she pulled back the hood and a crown of blond waves tumbled out around her slim shoulders. She was a little taller than Trinity but twice as thin.

"You're the couple who looked after Belinda," she said.

"Belinda," Trinity murmured. "That's a pretty name."

"We called her Bonnie," Zack said. "It means 'happy.' 'Pretty.'"

The girl's blue eyes sparkled as she shoved her hands into her sweater's pockets. "She smiled at me the first time at six weeks. She hasn't stopped since." Her expression firmed as she rolled back her shoulders. "I wanted you to know I never meant to lose her. I wanted to tell you it was an accident."

Zack exhaled. "That's some accident."

"And I didn't mean to get pregnant, if you want to know—" her chin and tone lowered "—but I never regretted for a moment bringing Bel into this world."

Trinity asked, "What about the father?"

"That's where I was headed that afternoon. Ryan never knew about my pregnancy until after Bel was born. He doesn't have a mom and his dad…" The girl's gaze dropped away. "Well, he's away a lot."

"And your own parents?"

"My dad left a long time ago. Mom's not happy with me." She shrugged. "What's new? From the very first day she told me I should give Bel up. She said it'd be easier that way."

Trinity made an anguished, barely audible noise and Zack held her firm.

"That day my mom had been at me again," the girl went on. "She said I couldn't stay there anymore. It was costing her too much. I wasn't paying my keep. So I decided to pack some stuff and Bel and catch a bus into town. I was going to get a connecting ride to my boyfriend's place. He'd moved to Wyoming. When we got to the bus stop, though, it started to snow. I had to get Bel out of the weather so I left my suitcase to walk over and ask that cabdriver how much it'd cost to get to the bus depot in town. But he was moving inside the store, getting something hot to drink or eat, I guess. It was really cold by then and the snow was falling harder. I put Bel inside the cab and hurried back to the stop to get my case. I was crossing back when the cab pulled away." Her eyes glazed over and Zack knew she was reliving that moment. "I ran after them up the road, but he didn't stop. I ran until I couldn't run anymore."

Trinity asked, "But you didn't tell anyone?"

"I rang Bel's father but he wasn't home and wasn't picking up his cell, either. I didn't have a choice. I had to go back to Mom. I was crying and shaking. She put me to bed and promised she'd phone the police. When we hadn't heard anything by the next day, she admitted she hadn't made the call at all. So I did."

A tear dropped down her cheek and the girl's throat bobbed on a swallow at the same time Trinity bowed her head and groaned. Zack's hold around Trinity's waist tightened. A maternal grandmother as good as disowning her own granddaughter. The situation must have sounded alarmingly close to her own.

"I wanted you to know that I love Bel. I've only ever wanted what's best for her." The baby's mother slipped the hood back over her head. "Sometimes it's just hard to figure things out."

Zack was moved. But feeling sorry for this girl didn't help the baby.

"Where are you staying now?"

"Ms. Cassidy organized a place in a shelter. There's heaps of support there."

"If you need anything…" Zack proceeded to give out his full name, and where and how to find him. "Don't forget, okay?"

More tears filled her eyes as the girl-mother looked at them both almost questioningly. "I'm glad you were the ones to find her. You seem like a really nice couple."

Trinity stood, stunned, as the girl jogged back and the police car, with little Bonnie—Belinda—drove away. She didn't take her eyes off the vehicle until it was a speck in the distant forest of trees. Zack didn't move or talk, either. It was as if all the energy in their personal world was suddenly captured and taken away.

It was bad enough having to hand over that defenseless child to a person who didn't look old enough to have graduated high school. In her more rational mind Trinity knew there must be wonderful, devoted and *careful* teen moms who didn't lose their babies…who had support and didn't need to act impulsively. But this young mother had less than no help.

The only word for little Bel's grandmother was *heartless.* No, there were two more words. Selfish and negligent. How was it that Trinity had been more than willing to care for that baby when she'd never laid eyes on her before, when there was no previous attachment, and yet a woman who should have no hesitation in giving her own life to protect had failed so miserably in the "decent human being" department? Hell, even Zack, with his mercenary reputation, had stepped up to act honorably.

Trinity had never been able to get her head around her own grandparents' dismissal of their own flesh and blood. It didn't compute that basic instinct shouldn't override other considerations like social shame or disappointment. Where were their compassion and love? As a baby, there'd been none for her from her maternal grandmother, none for this baby, either. And the pain was so great, squeezing and tearing at her heart that Trinity felt as if she was right there in the backseat of that police car, too, looking out over a span of uncertain years all over again.

What if something happened to Bel's mother? That baby would have no one and Trinity would never know. She'd be in the dark about that baby's future for the rest of her life.

And she didn't know if she could bear it.

When another car came into sight, heading up the lonely road, Trinity didn't pay it any mind. But the late model SUV turned into Zack's driveway and a lady with neat silver-blond hair and a chic woolen pantsuit slipped out of the driver's side door.

Zack's arm slid away from around her waist; she'd only been half aware of it being there but now she missed the support… the warmth. The cool of the morning seeped in, sending shivers scuttling over her skin. As the visitor neared, she slapped her thighs at the same time Cruiser strolled over to join her, his tail wagging low between his legs.

"There you are, you bad boy." The woman patted Cruiser's head then addressed Zack. "Has he been much trouble?"

Although he felt like his gut was on the floor after watching that police car drive away, Zack did his best to welcome his neighbor. Last night before dinner, he'd thought to leave a message on the Dales' phone, letting them know where to find their dog when they got back. Mrs. Dale was here now to collect Cruiser. Take him home.

And then there were two.

He thought he'd be relieved when the "lost baby" situation was settled...when this monster of a dog was out of his house. But he didn't feel relieved. Zack felt more hollow than he ever had in his life.

"Mrs. Dale," he said, "this is Trinity Matthews."

Mrs. Dale's smile broadened. "Lovely to meet you."

Zack explained, "He showed up here yesterday morning."

"When Jim and I went out the other afternoon, we left him on a long lead outside. We expected to be back by early evening but that storm held us up. When we got back, we found the lead chewed through and no Cruiser anywhere to be seen. Since the weather's eased up, we've searched around. We called all the folks around with kids. I told you how much he's drawn to children. I never thought to call here."

Trinity glanced over at Zack but he didn't bother to explain to Mrs. Dale about the baby. He merely hunkered down and when Cruiser waddled over, he caught his big hairy face, smiled and said, "Guess this is your lift."

Cruiser whined out a growl, his backside wobbling as his tail wagged harder.

Crossing her arms, Mrs. Dale pegged out a leg. "Zack, dear, I think you've made a friend."

"He's made one, too." Zack pushed to his feet.

Mrs. D's head slanted as she spoke to Trinity. "Are you staying for a few days?" She examined the sky. "The weather's cleared up beautifully."

"Actually I'm on my way back East."

"Don't tell me. New York? Too busy for my liking, but home is home."

Mrs. Dale thanked Zack again and after Trinity gave his neck a big hug, obedient as always, Cruiser followed Mrs. Dale back to her car. She opened the tailgate and a moment later, another member of their quartet was whisked away.

Trinity began to shiver again and this time she couldn't seem to stop. Zack brought his arm around her shoulder. "Come in out of the cold."

"I'm not cold."

"Come in for coffee then. I sure need one."

Noting the fallen tree trunk blocking the front entrance as they passed, Trinity followed as he headed toward the back of the cabin. Even with the shivering, she would rather have stood out here awhile longer although, of course, there was no chance the baby was ever coming back. She knew Bonnie—Belinda—wasn't hers. Wasn't theirs. Still, she felt as if a slice had been taken out of her heart.

Inside, Zack put on the pot while, feeling numb, she took a seat on a stool at the counter.

As he fished the milk out of the fridge, Zack commented, "She seems like a nice girl."

"*Girl* being the operative word." A withering feeling coursed through her and Trinity had to close her eyes to, in some way, try to contain it. "With a mother like that, how's she ever supposed to get ahead?"

"I'm sure she'll manage."

Trinity supposed *she* had. But she also knew how tough and long that road was. Someone of Zack's background would have no idea what a hard slog "going it alone" could be. So...

"What if she doesn't manage?"

He set down the milk and cast her a comforting look. "I gave her my contact details. We can't do anything more than that."

"Can't we?" Surely there must be *something*.

His brow furrowing, he crossed over. "What are you saying?"

"It shouldn't be too difficult to find out her name and address."

"That's not the way this is supposed to work. Mother and child are reunited. I know it doesn't look ideal, but I thought you'd be pleased."

"I am." Her heart sank more, her shoulders slumped and

Trinity lowered her voice. "I just want to keep an eye out. Maybe babysit sometime."

"From *New York?*"

She grunted and swung away. She didn't want to hear rational arguments. She wanted to be there. To help.

When he went back to making coffee, she moved to the windows and the view that had once seemed so private but now only looked…lonely. She hugged herself but her body seemed to have lost all its heat. She couldn't imagine ever feeling truly warm again.

She muttered more to herself than to Zack, "You could never understand."

She heard a cup hit the counter, his footsteps falling on the timber, coming closer. Then he was behind her and, hands on her shoulders, he spun her around. His jaw was tight and nostrils were flared the barest amount as if that might help curb the emotion she saw flashing in his eyes.

"You're upset now," he said calmly enough. "We need to sit down and let this all settle in. This ended the way it was always supposed to—baby and mother reunited."

Stinging emotion crept up the back of Trinity's throat. "I can't help thinking we should do more."

"Trinity, *it's not our place.*" While she recoiled, he scrubbed a hand down his face and sucked in a breath. "In a couple of days, you'll begin to see. You need to let her go."

One part of her knew he was right. They'd played out whatever part fate had laid in their path. Now they had to move on. But how did a person move on when they felt stuck? All she could see was Bonnie's smiling face. All she could hear was that little girl's laughter. Then she thought of that young mother's mountain of problems. It made her feel physically ill.

But as Zack brought her near and rubbed her back as he

leaned his cheek lightly on her head, she told herself: *he's right. Of course, he's right.*

That baby—*their* baby—had always belonged to someone else.

Ten

Trinity didn't want to stay for breakfast. She didn't want to stay, period.

So after they'd showered and were properly dressed, he relented and called a cab. But he insisted on accompanying her to the airport. He'd wanted to wait until she was booked on a flight, but she was just as insistent that he needed to plow on with this day.

Get on with his life.

After his "we need to let it go" speech, guess he'd asked for it.

He kissed her goodbye outside the terminal but the caress was as different to last night's as today's blue sky was to the previous gray. Their lips didn't linger, her smile wasn't convincing and as she walked away, it was all he could do not to drag her back and demand that she stay until they'd found some way to make their peace. Get beyond this somehow.

Instead he watched her disappear into a building thrumming with a backlog of folk needing to make up for the lost time that freak snowstorm had created. He wasn't aware how long he stood there, watching, thinking, before the cabbie wound down the window and gave him a verbal prod.

"Where to next, sir?"

Zack glanced back. Where to, indeed.

He slid into the back passenger seat and gave a Denver city address.

Trinity arrived in New York later that day feeling exhausted but unwilling to delay taking action on the decision she'd made during the hours spent waiting at the airport and during the flight back home.

Now she slid out of the cab and headed through the automatic glass sliding door of the familiar downtown building remembering how that word—*home*—had tugged at her heartstrings for as long as she could recall. She'd worked hard to put herself through college and find the wherewithal to move from Ohio, to get away. She'd never forget her exhilaration when she'd been awarded a position with *Story*. Her apartment in Brooklyn was tiny but she'd filled it with bits and pieces that made her happy—paintings by talented new artists, books that were favorites and felt like old friends.

But that apartment wasn't *hers*. Wasn't truly home.

As she thumbed a foyer elevator button, she could admit that those walls and neighbors had only ever felt temporary. She would never tell Zack although she thought perhaps he'd guessed: despite her initial disapproval of him, his cabin in the woods had felt more like a safe haven than any address she'd known.

But that time was over. After their amazing night together, Zack had said he wanted to keep in touch. But something wiser than blind hope said he wouldn't call. She didn't blame him. He had a brilliant life with concrete goals, as well as family and friends and associates to keep him company whenever he felt the urge. He didn't need her moodiness and baggage bringing down his party. And, honestly, she didn't need him, either. She had a plan.

As Trinity moved out of the elevator, nodded a greeting to the receptionist on her way to Kate's office, she knew precisely what she needed to do. She'd never felt more determined, anxious—*right* in her life. Today was the beginning of all her best tomorrows.

"I know I said I'd get Dirkins to sign," Zack said. "I haven't given up yet."

Thomas sat on the right-hand side of the mile-long conference table, elbows on chair arms and fingers steepled as he watched his older brother pace the length of the Harrison Plaza District office suite. Zack knew he must look like a caged jungle cat because that's precisely how he felt. Since he'd arrived back from Colorado two days ago, he hadn't been able to settle into anything, including coming any nearer to closing that Denver deal.

He'd thought about Trinity's suggestion, putting forward an offer of a partnership of co-ownership to Dirkins. Although a big part of Zack wanted to help the older man out if he could, that simply wasn't the way he did business. Equal equity meant disputes down the track. Any weakening of the Harrison foundation—even in a small way—was anathema to his motto.

Stay calm, stay focused and succeed.

With his father floating in and out of the office and his brothers happy with nine-to-five, someone had to man the bow.

"Maybe we should let the deal slide," Thomas said. "Since Mom and Dad had their split, he's not nearly as hell-bent on soaring through this economic downturn. Not that their break is permanent," he added.

Really? Who said it wasn't?

"Our family's not invincible, Thomas. We all just like to pretend that it is."

The steepled fingers lowered. "Where's this coming from?

You've been a royal pain in the butt since getting back from Colorado. You did nothing but frown and growl at Nicki's school play last night. What the hell happened out there?"

"Nothing of consequence."

"Every time I ask about those female guests you had holed up in your cabin, you fob me off. Now I'm telling you, I want to know." Thomas swore. "Is someone *blackmailing* you?"

Zack moved to the wall-to-wall windows. "Don't be melodramatic."

"From what you told me, that actress you were seeing wanted to test those waters."

"And I told her where to get off. If she wants to spread rumors about cracks in the Harrison family camp, she can try her hardest. No one rattles me. Nothing gets under my skin."

"I'd always thought so, but clearly something or someone is screwing with your *cool and composed* gauge big-time."

Thomas crossed to where Zack was staring out over a panoramic view of Midtown that normally never failed to inspire. Colorado was relaxing but this was where he thrived. Where the real opportunities lived.

"We're more than brothers. We're friends. Talk to me." Thomas set a hand on Zack's shoulder. "Let me help."

Zack tried to ignore the empty feeling funneling through his middle. He muttered, "You'd never believe it."

"Try me."

After another moment of indecision, Zack moved over to a chair and spent the next fifteen minutes divulging the top points of his most recent stay in Colorado. Thomas looked surprised when he described how he'd found the baby. He'd looked stunned when he'd said he'd offered to bring her home until the authorities could take over. He talked about Cruiser and what an intelligent, responsible, *big* dog he was.

Mostly he talked about Trinity. He even admitted how close they'd grown. He recalled how Trinity had described the feeling when she'd put down Bonnie—*Bel*—after caring for her nonstop. Now it was like some part of *him* was missing.

"I've never felt so edgy in my life." Zack threw up his hands and got to his feet. "Obviously the isolation played tricks on my mind. I identified with my captor. What's that called?" He snapped his fingers. "Stockholm Syndrome."

Thomas looked amused. "It was *your* home. I imagine your rules."

Zack held his brow then wiped the damp away. "I must be sick."

"Absolutely. *Heartsick.* Zack, buddy, sounds like you're in love."

Zack stared hard at the younger man then coughed out a raucous laugh. His brothers were always on him about finding Miss Right. They never let up.

"Trin and I were together *two days*." He held up as many fingers to accentuate the point.

"Sometimes that's all it takes. I knew I wanted to marry Willa after our first date. Dylan knew Rhian only a week."

"I'm different. I've always been different."

Thomas sat back in his chair and steepled his fingers again, and Zack remembered his little brother had once wanted to be a psychologist. He might be a touch off course, but he sure didn't need to suffer a bad imitation of Freud.

Thomas asked, "What are you so afraid of?"

Zack set his hands low on his hips. "For one, falling in love is not in my plans."

"Those plans being...?"

"To take over Harrison Hotels. Dad's practically set to retire."

"And the rest of us lost our brains the moment we said 'I do' and had kids."

Zack arched a brow. "Let's be honest. You all have different priorities."

"Our families. Damn right. Doesn't mean we can't run a business."

"If Dad had spent more time with Mom, they wouldn't be going through this separation now. He should have slowed down five, ten years ago when the cracks started to show."

"Zack, that's not your place."

That pulled him up. He remembered saying the same words to Trinity when she wanted to get involved more with the baby after she'd gone. He'd tried to make her see reason but the truth was she'd been closer to the real heart of that situation than he'd been, like he felt closer to his parents' problems than his younger brother, or any of the others, for that matter.

Thomas was still talking. "And I'm here to tell you that a man *can* have both—a family of his own as well as a fulfilling professional life."

"Not without sacrifices."

"Life is all about sacrifices. Or it should be. Believe me, that's when we really start to reap the rewards."

"Like endless 3:00 a.m. feedings?"

"Sounds as if you can handle it."

"How about apologizing over and over for getting home late from meetings?"

"If you're smart, and devoted, you can organize your time. What are you trying to prove? You don't have to sell your soul and make a billion or three to be happy."

No one seemed to get it! "It's how I see myself. Calm. Focused. Eye forever on the horizon."

"One could conjecture they're fine qualities for a husband and father."

Zack didn't know about that. But, after this conversation, one thing was clear. He wouldn't be able to rest—to think straight—until he saw Trinity again. If she was going through anything like the torture he'd known these past days, she'd need to lay her own cards on the table and see him, too.

And he happened to have the perfect night in mind.

Eleven

Trinity was about to leave for the day when a special delivery arrived—a small box wrapped in white gloss paper. The label was addressed: *Trinity Matthews. Careful. Fragile.* The deliveryman said he'd been instructed to wait for a response.

While the man gave her some privacy and ducked outside the reception room door, from the reception counter, Narelle Johns popped her perfectly coiffed, titian-blond head up.

"You were on your way out, Trin. I'll take care of that, if you want."

Trinity received goods from many of the people she interviewed—merchandise ranging from beauty products to quaint artworks to scented soaps resembling flags of the world. But as she weighed this particular gift, she felt most curious. She rotated the box and read the return label.

She murmured aloud, *"From Mr. Poultry-geist."*

Her stomach looped and perspiration broke down the line of her back. She had to find the nearest chair or chance rubber legs buckling beneath her. Seeing her reaction, Narelle shoved back her caster chair and zoomed over.

"Are you all right? Do you want a glass of water? Do I need to get security?"

"No, no. It's nothing like that."

"Then why do you look like you've seen a ghost?"

Trinity thought of Zack's chicken story and her lips wobbled on a smile. "In a way, I have."

Narelle pulled up a nearby chair. With no one else in the room, Trinity found she couldn't contain her curiosity enough to wait until she got home, or even make it back to her office. With the receptionist looking on, she peeled back the red ribbon, tore open the iridescent white paper, pried open the fitted lid and pulled out...

Narelle let out a rapt sigh. "OMG. It's *beautiful*."

Moisture edged Trinity's eyes as she studied the thin glass ball that seemed to tell so many stories.

"A snow globe," she murmured, tipping the ball, which was set on a gold stand, upside-down then right-side-up. Her smile widened as a flurry of snow fell and settled on the scene. There was a wood cabin—nothing near as extravagant as Zack's but just as homey looking—a big dog standing on his hind legs, perhaps barking at, or catching snow in his mouth. A couple stood by the front door. In the woman's arms lay a baby swaddled in a white wrap.

Trinity screwed her eyes shut and swallowed deeply. Looking into that globe brought to the surface such a mix of emotions—feelings she'd fought to control these past days but never to forget. She wanted those memories to live on in her mind until the day she died. Still, she didn't want to live in the past, not anymore. She'd already decided to take Zack's advice and move forward.

"Who's it from?" Narelle had picked up the box and was peering and digging around inside. "I don't remember anyone we've interviewed having a connection with snow globes."

"It's personal."

"In that case, you'd better read this note."

Trinity took the folded piece of notepaper from Narelle and scanned the lines. Every word made her heart lift a little higher and her resolve dig in a little deeper.

Narelle asked, "Are you going to go?"

Trinity darted a look at the younger woman who'd been reading over her shoulder.

Narelle shrugged. "I couldn't help but pick up on a few phrases, like 'need to see you again' and 'this Saturday night.'"

Trinity admitted, "When I was snowed-in in Colorado, I stayed in a place something like this."

"A wood cabin? With a dog?"

Trinity nodded.

But then Narelle tipped closer, squinted into the globe. "Isn't that a baby?"

"Yes, it is."

The receptionist sat back. "Wow. For a minute I thought this guy might've had this specially made."

"I think he did."

"But, a *baby?*"

"Believe me, it's a long story." One she'd told Kate but no one else.

"I guess the only question is…" Narelle waggled her eyebrows. "Are you going to accept?" She glanced again at the note, now lying open on Trinity's lap. "Says it's an engagement party. Black-tie at a private address in Oyster Bay Cove. All sounds terribly romantic."

Gnawing her lower lip, Trinity tipped the globe up and righted it again. The snow drifted down, coating the scene, and in her mind she could hear Cruiser barking, Bonnie Bel laughing and Zack…

She sighed.

He was intelligent and strong and funny and knowing him the way she did now—not the way the press depicted him—

she couldn't help but miss him. At night, alone in her bed, she could still feel his warmth, his soul-lifting kiss.

On that final night, he'd said he wanted to see her again. The more time had gone by, the less she'd believed that he had. But it seemed he was as good as his word and, of course, she needed to accept, if only to tell him how that experience in Colorado had changed her life and why she could never see him again. Trinity sent word back. She accepted his invitation but she would make her own way to his parents' estate.

When Zack received her reply, he'd reached for his cell to call her. He had *Story Magazine*'s office number, and if she'd left for the day, he'd also searched out and had on quick dial her private line details. But, twenty-four hours later, as he stood in his parents' home overlooking the sound, he was glad he'd refrained. If she wanted to find her own way here, no harm. As long as she accepted that he would drive her home, and not until morning.

Feeling a tap on his dinner jacket's shoulder, he angled around. His mother, dressed in an elegant cream pantsuit, had left off entertaining the guests long enough to check on her middle child.

"I swear you've been standing staring out this window for an hour. Are you sure this girl is coming?"

"She'll be here."

"There's so many interesting ladies asking about you. Your sister does have a lot of lovely friends."

"And given it's Sienna and her fiancé's party, I'm happy to leave the mingling and small talk to her."

His mother's green eyes glistened much like the emeralds dangling from her ears. "That's unlike you, Zackery. You're usually so amenable."

Leaning forward, Zack brushed a kiss on his dear mother's cheek. "I'm fine. Go and enjoy yourself."

Disappointment and confusion lining her still beautiful face, she moved off to rejoin her many guests. Through the library door, Zack caught sight of his father cutting her off at the pass. He was offering to top up her champagne but clearly he wanted to talk, to stay close. Zack could imagine his mother's thoughts.

Where were you all those nights *I* wanted to talk?

She'd been left largely to bring up the children while the man of the house had basked in the glory that was Harrison Hotels. They'd come together twice a year for vacations and his father usually made all the important dates in his kids' lives. But as Zack had grown older he'd come to appreciate how lonely his mother must have been all those evenings her husband had stayed late at the office…the many weekends he'd worked out of town.

They never argued in front of the children, but there'd been a couple of midnight quarrels Zack had overheard. Accusations with ugly words bandied around like "adultery" and "divorce." As a boy, he'd flung the covers up over his head and prayed for his parents to stay together. But he never believed his father had ever cheated unless his mistress was his office and career.

As the couple walked together into the mansion's main reception lounge where a small band was playing and the party was in full swing, Zack returned his focus to the view outside one of the private library's tall arched windows. He hoped his parents worked it out, but he would understand if they didn't. His father had *tried* his best; his mother had, too. But if a man wanted to become a corporate force to be reckoned with, no matter what Thomas said, there simply weren't enough hours in the day.

The swinging arc of car lights on the driveway had Zack thrusting back his shoulders. When he confirmed the vehicle was a cab, he strode out to meet the likely occupant. A moment later, near the front door, he cleared his throat and told Keats, their regular doorman for special events, that he would greet this guest himself.

Out on the extensive portico, Zack rubbed his hands together against the slight chill in the air while the cabdriver held open the back passenger door and Trinity Matthews alighted.

She wore his favorite color on her—a deep vibrant red. The dress was silky and two hundred percent sexy with silver brocade crisscrossing the bodice and looping around her neck. A luminous lightweight wrap rested in the crooks of her arms, its tails lifting softly in the breeze either side of the shapely high-waist-to-heel sheath.

When she saw him, her eyes rounded before she gathered herself and, shifting the wrap up around her bare shoulders, clutched her silver pocketbook close to her chest. He'd heard about women looking like veritable visions. Now he could take pleasure in that wonder himself.

As he moved forward, she seemed to take a breath and moved forward, too. When they stopped, standing face-to-face, he covered her chilled hands in his. He wanted to circle her in his arms and generate some heat the way they did best. Instead he smiled into her gorgeous moonlit eyes and led her into his family's home.

Trinity had been ready for affluence but this magnificent waterfront estate was almost beyond imagination. The driveway had wound on forever. The house—more a mansion!—exuded an elegant yesteryear charm with an architectural design that reminded her of those old larger-than-life black-and-white films.

"This makes my studio apartment look like a shoebox," she said as, his hand on her elbow, Zack led her up a wide arc of stone steps. "When was it built?"

"Nineteen thirty-six. With ten acres to romp around on, it was great here growing up, but seven bedrooms and an equal number of full baths, along with a library, ballroom, office, plus, plus, plus… It's too big for my parents now."

"They're thinking of selling?"

"That's still to be decided."

Inside, a three-tiered crystal chandelier hung from the soaring ceiling of a majestic vestibule. Artwork on the walls looked as if they might belong in a museum. She guessed the trimmings were all twenty-four-karat-gold plating, at least.

With that dynamite smile that never failed to leave her lightheaded, Zack urged her along.

"Come in and meet the family."

Family...

The very word made Trinity's stomach jump so high, she had to press a palm to help slow the knots. Logically she had nothing to fear. From all she'd heard, the Harrisons were a great bunch. And their obvious wealth didn't put her off. It was the fact she'd come at Zack's invitation—as his date—and she was expecting everyone to be suitable, curious and ask a slew of questions.

She'd already decided to be her usual vague self where private matters and the past were concerned. She was certain Zack would understand. But she intended to soak up this atmosphere and the conversation tonight. After spending those days in Colorado, she was curious like she'd never been before about seeing a truly happy family in action.

"Are the children here?" she asked as they moved beneath a soaring ornate carved wood archway and the live music grew louder.

"Wouldn't be a party without the munchkins. Although they'll be put to bed at a reasonable hour."

"In one of the seven bedrooms," she concluded.

But, taking her wrap and handing it to a uniformed maid, he shook his head. "There are a couple of private guesthouses on the grounds in case any of us decide to stay over but also want our own space."

"Are you staying over tonight?"

"Oh, yes." He sent her a lopsided grin. "So are you."

Trinity almost swallowed her tongue. Before she could object, she was standing among other guests and Zack was handing her a flute of champagne while introducing her to an inquisitive-looking man who resembled Zack a great deal. Same raven's-wing hair. Same dazzling smile.

"Thomas, this is Trinity Matthews."

Thomas took her hand and dipped his head in greeting. "So glad you could make it. It's not every day our little sister accepts a marriage proposal." He flicked a glance Zack's way. "That leaves one." He called over to a curvy redhead whose smile was as big as her generous bosom. "Willa, sweetheart, come meet Trinity, Zack's date."

Willa was there in a heartbeat. "We've heard all about you. Being stuck in Zack's cabin, cut off from everything."

Trinity waited for her to mention the baby. But Willa only talked on about the recent freakish weather. Clearly Zack hadn't divulged *that* much about their story, although she did catch Thomas looking at her thoughtfully. She knew the siblings were close. Were Thomas and Zack close enough to discuss the more intimate details of the night they'd spent together?

After five minutes of chatting, Zack called another woman over. She wore an amazing peach-colored evening gown. Her brunette hair was swept up in a flattering loose-curl style.

"This," Zack said, "is Sienna, my baby sister and woman of the hour."

"Congratulations on your engagement," Trinity said, subtlety checking Sienna's hands, not for the engagement ring so much as those chewed nails carried over from her childhood. "You must be very happy."

"I'm *beyond* happy! And a little shocked. I only accepted David's proposal on the weekend. Mom insisted on putting this bash together. You know how mothers are."

While Trinity kept her straight face, Zack explained the engagement situation.

"They've only known each other four weeks—"

"Three," Sienna cut in. "We met during a chocolate-making workshop in Brussels, although we ate more pralines than we made. Then we went on to Amsterdam together, then Berlin, then home. David's from New York, too." Sienna laughed. "We had to go halfway around the world to meet and fall in love."

Trinity held her brow. "Your heads must be spinning."

"It's strange," Sienna said. "I guess I knew I'd do it one day. Tie the knot, I mean. It's in the Harrison DNA. But now I so totally get what people mean about love at first sight."

Trinity was intrigued. "You knew you were going to be married the first time you laid eyes on each other?"

"It wasn't so much a 'club to the head' deal. It wasn't as if I imagined a big gold ring the instant we met. Just somewhere deep inside, I knew we'd be together." Her earnest look faded and she laughed again. "Sounds silly, doesn't it? My cool, collected brother here wouldn't buy it for a second. Although I'm betting sparks flew when the two of you met."

Sienna was about to expand on that point when a woman—clearly a good friend—grabbed her free hand and unceremoniously dragged her away to another circle of people. No sooner had Zack's sister left than another brother and sister-in-law introduced themselves as well as one of their children.

As they spoke about the handmade toys Zack kept at the cabin, Trinity found herself relaxing in a way she never had before. It must be her imagination but she felt connected to these people who came from perfect backgrounds and seemed to lead such charmed lives. What a wonderful dream come true to really belong to all this.

She was introduced to Zack's mother and father separately, as well as a myriad of other people whose names she could never hope to remember. Zack was a perfect host and the hours sped by. When the music's volume dropped and guests began to leave, Trinity couldn't believe the time she caught on her wristwatch.

"It's past twelve."

Zack's fingertips slid down her bare arm. "If your name's not Cinderella, I don't see a problem."

"But the night... It went so quickly."

"These big family occasions usually do. By the time you get through speaking to everyone, the staff is already tidying up." Zack ducked a look around her shoulder. "But there is someone you haven't met yet."

He beckoned a man over. Again, the family resemblance couldn't be mistaken. This must be the eldest brother.

"Dylan, Trinity Matthews," Zack said.

Trinity extended her hand but was a little taken aback when Dylan shook with his left rather than right hand. As the brothers talked, including her in the conversation wherever possible, Trinity couldn't help noticing Dylan's right jacket sleeve hung and its flat cuff was tucked into the pocket. He was an amputee? How long ago had the accident happened? Or was it a birth defect?

A woman joined them, waving a hand full of diamonds. She addressed Trinity.

"Hi, I'm Rhian, and I've come to rescue you from these two. They've been known to talk past dawn when they get started."

Dylan spoke behind his good hand. "She's always bossing me around."

Rhian play-growled. "Oh, you love it."

Dylan shrugged. "She's right. I do. Are you staying over tonight? We can do breakfast." He spoke to Trinity. "The kids love Nana's pancakes."

Rhian knuckled her husband's ribs. "So do you. But we need to say good-night now if we're going to get up at the crack of dawn."

"Do you jog together?" Trinity couldn't think of another reason—any reason—for getting up that early.

Dylan explained. "When the sun rises, so does our youngest. Rhian drags herself out of bed Monday through Friday so—rain, hail or shine—I take the weekend shift."

They each said good-night and before anyone else could sidle up, Zack took her hand and headed for a doorway. Not

the enormous carved-wood arch this time, but a far less osten-
tatious exit that took them down a dimly lit hall.

Trotting on his heels, she asked, "Where are we going?"

"Home."

"What do you mean, *home?*"

He stopped abruptly and she was pulled up in her tracks. In
the shadows, she felt his gaze burning into hers, felt his will
reaching out and wrapping around her, strong and warm like
a snug cocoon she couldn't hope to escape.

"I told you when you arrived," he murmured dangerously
close to her lips. "Tonight you're staying with me."

Trinity balked. *And I don't have a say?*

But when she opened her mouth to object—because she'd
always meant to object, hadn't she?—he took the opportunity,
as she should have known he would. He locked an arm around
her waist, dragged her near and then he kissed her until the
space they occupied was spinning and all thoughts other than
submission shot like a round of fireworks out of her mind.

Twelve

They went out the back door where his car was parked and waiting. A few minutes down a winding private road then he was opening her passenger side door again and they were hurrying like teenagers into his private villa overlooking the water.

The moment they were inside and the door was shut, he took her in his arms and, running his hands over her bare shoulders, down her back, he kissed her again like he'd been dying to do all evening. When his mouth finally left hers, his breathing was labored. So was hers.

"It killed me to play polite host all night and not drag you away sooner."

"You were so sure that I'd come."

He unclasped the strap at her nape. "I knew I could convince you."

When the gown dropped to her feet, her eyes glittered up into his before she stepped out of the silky puddle at her feet and kicked it aside. Naked but for a pair of skimpy silk panties, she smiled like a cat about to get her cream.

She murmured, "So start convincing."

Every drop in his veins heated to a point long past stable. He swept her up off her feet and strode to the main bedroom.

He'd left instructions for the bed to be turned down and candles to be lit at midnight. She was looking adoringly into his eyes, curving her palm around his cheek as he set her purposefully down on the bed. But unlike the last time, she didn't lie back quietly. Rather she brought herself upright until she was kneeling on the side of the bed before him. Then she reached up and stud by stud undid his shirt while he tried to keep it together enough to roll his shoulders out of his jacket and tossed it aside. He heeled off his shoes at the same time she concentrated to release the cummerbund then the catch at the top of his trousers.

And every second, he watched from above…. The way her beautiful body moved and swayed as she worked to undress him. How her soft skilled hands drove up over his bare chest once his shirt was set aside. All night her scent had near driven him wild…light and flowery and at the same time sensual. *Sexy.* While she'd spoken with guests, he'd imagined her getting ready for tonight, dabbing pulse points with a long, thin stick of perfume…behind her ears, on her wrists, between her breasts, across her bikini line.

When he stood before her wearing nothing but socks, she crouched in front of him and, without fair warning, guided his heavy erection into her mouth.

He was no stranger to sex. He'd enjoyed many women and in every way possible. But he'd never been lifted to this bone-melting place before. As her nails dragged up over his scrotum and her head bobbed down farther, he couldn't be certain he'd last the distance. Closing his eyes, he combed his fingers through her long, silken hair while, second by second, both their movements grew—and to a crucial point where all too soon he had to ease away.

"I like what you do to me." He groaned. "In fact, I like it a little too much."

Her eyes in the muted light were liquid. Her smile was nothing short of pure sin. As she rolled back, he caught the slim bands of her panties and silently thanked her when she lifted her legs so he could peel them off the rest of the way. When she put out her arms to him, he positioned himself between her open, bent knees. Holding onto her thighs, he drank in the sight of her while the tide inside him swirled and climbed even higher.

He found the condom wrap on the side table. When he was sheathed, he cupped the back of her neck and claimed another kiss while he pushed forward and at last entered her. He forced himself to go slow and build the rhythm. But the way she was kissing him back—so hungry and deep—it wasn't long before he was left balanced on the brink. He murmured against her lips, "God, I missed you."

"I didn't think you'd call."

"I was an idiot to wait this long."

She smiled against his lips. "Your invitation arrived two days after I got back."

"Like I said…" He nipped her lower lip. "Too long."

When she gripped his hips and wound her legs around the back of his thighs, his every thought and fiber zeroed in on raw, scorching sensation. He felt on fire, inside and out, and as his rhythm increased, she let him know with her sighs and her moves that she was already almost there, too.

The burn was too good. Her mouth nibbling his, too sweet. As she began to tremble and clutch around him, Zack's mind fogged then went a perfect high-pitched blank. The earth began to shudder as he stilled, and in that stellar, precise fragment in time, he knew.

If he ever fell in love, he'd want it to feel just like this…just like Trin… "I love your family."

They were lying quietly, enjoying the afterglow of their lovemaking while Trinity drew aimless patterns through the hair on Zack's chest. The occasional distant blow of a ship's horn and the wash of ancient branches over the roof were lulling. But she'd enjoyed her evening so much, she'd simply had to let him know.

Now he asked, "You didn't feel overwhelmed?"

"Maybe a little, but only in a nice way. Do you mind me asking…? How did Dylan lose his arm?"

"A car knocked him off his bike when he was twelve. His right arm was caught beneath the tire. The main nerves were severed. He lost all movement and the limb withered. The arm's still attached but he can't use it."

"So Rhian met him after the accident…."

He craned up to give her an odd or protective look. "It doesn't make Dylan any less a human being. In fact, if anything, it makes him more a man. He still plays ball with his kids, makes them dinner, chases them around the yard. And he's a whiz with the company books. None of us even think about his arm anymore." He relaxed back down. "Dylan and Rhian will be together forever."

She believed him.

"Your mom was so welcoming," she said then. "And your dad's so funny. I know where you get your storytelling abilities from."

"They suit each other. That's what I think anyway."

"Who doesn't think that?"

"They're in the middle of discussions."

"About?"

"Whether to split."

"What? I don't believe it."

"It's been coming for a while. He's always spent a lot of time at the office, away on business. Last straw, she booked a Mediterranean cruise for just the two of them. At the eleventh hour Dad said he couldn't make it. Mom went on her own and when she came back, she wanted a separation. She brought us all together and explained that she'd raised her family and was beyond happy to be a grandmother but she also wanted some time with her husband before they were too old to enjoy one another. If he didn't agree, it was time to go their separate ways. Dad didn't think she was serious until she moved into their city apartment. She's made the social pages quite a few times on her own recently."

"So it's too late for a reconciliation?"

"I only know the writing was on the wall years ago."

"Personal and business don't mix?"

"Not when there are kids involved and the onus is placed on one parent to raise them. Not when you're talking billion-dollar turnovers that need to be met." He squeezed and tugged her up against him. "But that doesn't apply to you and me. We both have careers. Neither of us have kids." An awkward moment in which they both must have remembered Bonnie passed between them before he went on. "I want to see you again."

Trinity felt every one of her emotions condense and begin to glow. She'd enjoyed this evening. Even more, she'd enjoyed sharing Zack's bed again. But, unfortunately, that didn't change anything.

She moistened her lips. Took a breath.

"Zack, I can't see you after tonight."

His chest stopped moving then he asked, "You want me to prove how much you mean to me?" He rubbed the tip of his nose with hers. "I've been told I choose excellent gifts."

"You know that's not it."

"Then you liked the globe?"

"Of course I did. I meant to tell you a dozen times tonight only we never seemed to be alone. But I'm not here now because of a gift. I came because I needed to see you again."

He nuzzled against her neck. "And I needed to see you."

Her eyes began to burn. She thought she was ready for this conversation. But ready or not, she had to go on.

"I'll never forget those two days away. They changed me, Zack. Changed how I think about the world. About the future."

He rolled her over. "This is getting entirely too serious." But when his head slanted over hers, as difficult as it was to deny them both, she wound away and sat up.

He scratched his cheek and thought a moment.

"Okay," he finally said. "You want to talk. Let's talk."

She clutched the cover under her neck and admitted, "I don't want to hide from who I really am anymore. I had a tough time as a kid but I'm not going to let that beat me. I've decided. Someday I want a family of my own."

"A family...?" His brow and voice lowered. "Is this supposed to be some kind of ultimatum?"

"*No*. Never. You do whatever you want to do. Although I have to say, after seeing you tonight with your family, I think you might be hiding at least a part of who you really want to be, too."

He huffed. "Why is it so difficult to believe a man wants to commit to a career?"

She lifted a brow. "Some say careers are overrated. In fact, I quit my job when I flew back from Colorado."

His six-pack crunched as he sat up. "You love that job."

"I do. I *did*. But we get just one life. I want to work with kids. Maybe in counseling or shelters—"

"You're doing this to get in touch with Bonnie again," he cut in.

Her temper spiked. "Her name's Belinda. And you're wrong. I'm doing this because it's right for me, and I hope Bel and her mother find what's right for them, too."

His gaze held hers. "I don't believe you never want to feel this again."

"We want different things. I want more. Eventually marriage. A family. It's not a crime. Ask your brothers and sister." She sighed but didn't trust herself enough to touch and soothe away the crease cut between his brows. "It's just the way it is."

In the candlelight, she saw the determined glint in his eye. He didn't accept it. But for once, the decision wasn't up to him.

What she didn't say—what hurt the most—was in these few short days, she'd gone and done what, looking back on their time together, now seemed inevitable. She'd fallen in love.

As she'd lain awake at night thinking of all they'd shared during such a small vacuum in time, the realization had only grown. She was yet another Zack Harrison victim. She'd never feel for someone else the way she felt for him. If she wanted to fool herself, she could think about taking up his offer to continue their affair and hope that she'd be the one he'd end up with. Have a family with. But no matter how convincing this evening had been, truth was he must have been convincing with scores of other women before her.

"You'll spend the night," he finally said.

"Until dawn. I don't want to have pancakes with your family and give them the wrong impression."

"That we slept together?"

"That we're serious. Besides, I don't think a red evening gown is suitable attire for breakfast fare."

"I have sweaters in the closet."

She shook her head—was about to say the words—*No, Zack. No*—when his cell on the side table buzzed.

"You should answer it."

He growled. "I don't give a damn who it is."

"Maybe it's one of your brothers. Or your mother or father."

"They wouldn't call at this time of night—"

Her stomach pitched and she finished for him. "Unless something was wrong."

Turned out that the caller wasn't any part of his family. Wasn't work. It was the last person on earth either of them expected to hear from, particularly this late on a Saturday night.

Thirteen

On the other end of the line, Zack's caller took a halting breath then continued to explain her unhappy situation. When she was done, Zack asked, "Is there a motel nearby?"

He was given an establishment's name—she could see the motel's neon sign from where she stood making the call. Zack said he'd organize a room—not to worry about needing a card or cash—and he'd be there as soon as he could.

Already on his feet, heading for the walk-in closet for some jeans and a shirt, he terminated the call. He was thrusting his arms through the first button-down shirt he could grab when Trinity's shaky voice filtered across the room.

"Zack, you're scaring me. Who was that? What's wrong?"

"That girl. Bonnie's mother. Her name's Maggie. Maggie Lambert." He zipped up while collecting some running shoes. "She has the baby at a truck stop outside of Denver."

He heard something fall to the floor as she scrambled out of the bed. "Why? What happened?"

"I'll explain on the way. Here." He tossed her a shirt. "Put this on. *Hurry.*"

* * *

After stopping at her apartment so that she could change into traveling clothes, Zack called in a favor and organized a private emergency flight to Colorado. They arrived in the early hours of Sunday morning. The predawn was eerily dark and despite her overcoat, Trinity shivered as she alighted from the black Mercedes rental before he'd even shut down the purring engine.

Huddling into her coat, Trinity surveyed the motel, a rundown building with an erratically blinking blue neon sign. She flinched. "Are you sure this is the place?"

"Hardly five-star but better than hanging out in the early hours with an infant at a truck stop."

But when Zack roused the sleepy caretaker and the man rang through to Maggie's room—not once but three times—no one answered. Belinda and her mother were gone.

The long flight from New York to Denver had been nerve-racking enough. Now Trinity held her roiling stomach.

"What do we do now?"

"Call the police."

Trinity perked up. She'd half expected Zack to say there was nothing they could do. But if he hadn't offered to call the authorities, she would have phoned them herself. She couldn't rest without knowing that those two were safe. From the set of Zack's jaw, he felt the same way.

Moving out from the motel foyer back in the misty morning light, he stopped, found her gaze and firmly took her hand.

"We'll find them," he told her. "We won't leave until we do."

Unable to speak over the tears stinging her throat, Trinity nodded then gazed despairingly up and down the neon-blue-tinged road. Across the way was that truck stop. If Maggie had decided to catch a ride, she could be anywhere by now.

Zack had found his phone, presumably to contact the police, when a call came through. He frowned down at the screen before pressing the phone to his ear. "Hello?" He paused a moment then demanded, "Where the hell are you?"

A few seconds later, Zack ended the call.

"That was Maggie. Belinda woke early and wouldn't settle again so they went for a walk and ended up back over there."

He gestured toward the stop at the same time Trinity let loose that pent-up breath. They were here after all. *Thank God.*

Hand in hand, they strode across that road and in through the entrance of Big Bill's Burger Stop and Gas.

Inside, the café's chairs and booths were covered in worn red vinyl. The Formica tabletops shone, the aroma of coffee permeated the air and in a far corner a bereft young woman sat, waiting, a baby carrier perched beside her on the floor.

Trinity and Zack rushed over. She wanted to hug the girl, tell her they'd been so worried. But the words would sound judgmental and Zack had sounded annoyed enough just now on the phone. So instead Trinity forced a shaky smile and peered down at the baby while her heart leaped and sank at the same time.

The baby looked so peaceful, wonderfully oblivious to the turmoil surrounding her young, precious life. With all her being, Trinity wanted to lift her out of that carrier, hold her close to her heart and never let her go. Perhaps that was wrong. Bel wasn't hers but that maternal drive was so strong, she felt as if she were breaking inside.

Zack waited for her to slide into the booth then followed.

"We came as quickly as we could."

Maggie's face was drawn and her eyes glistened with unshed tears. She looked as if she'd trudged a thousand miles and had a thousand more to go.

"I'm sorry. I didn't mean for you to come all the way back out here. It's just—" Maggie shrugged those too-slim shoulders in her denim jacket "—I didn't know what else to do."

Zack prodded. "Tell us what happened."

"I spoke to Bel's dad on the phone late last week," Maggie began. "He said there were some great opportunities out where he was. That I should come out, too, and bring the baby. The people at the shelter were nice. We'd talked about me going to college. Getting a degree. But I thought he was inviting us. I thought he wanted to help take care of us."

When tears slipped down both Maggie's cheeks, Trinity felt her own throat throb with emotion. She reached across the table and held the girl's hand tight.

"I put together what money I had," Maggie said. "I left the shelter and called my mom to say we wouldn't be back. Then I phoned Ryan, Bel's dad, to set up times and stuff. He sounded…different." She seemed to look inward before her gaze lowered to her sleeping child. "I should've known. I got such a terrible feeling, but I went ahead and bought the ticket anyway then phoned again to tell him what time we'd be getting in. I so wanted it to work out." She bit her lower lip as her mouth bowed and more tears fell. "He hung up on me, but before he did, I heard a girl's voice in the background." Tears were spilling down her face now, curling around her quaking chin. "That's when I remembered your offer to help, Mr. Harrison—"

When he interrupted, Zack's voice was hoarse but also gentle. "Call me Zack."

Maggie nodded. "And Ms. Cassidy… She said what a lovely couple you were."

Zack blinked. "She did?"

"Uh-huh. But I already knew that. She had your number, the same one you told me that day when I got Bel back." A look of uncertainty and fear shuttered over her face. "I hope I'm doing the right thing."

Trinity squeezed Maggie's cool, bony hand. "Of course you are. We'll make sure you're both safe."

"But there's more," she said. "I've had so much time to think."

Trinity took a breath and waited.

"You both looked so torn up when I left with her that day," Maggie said, "and here you are, just like that, after a thirty-second phone call. I know you care about Bel. She's so easy to love." Maggie squirmed in her seat then, elbow on the table, she held her head. "This is the hardest thing I've ever had to say, to do, but I know in my heart that it's right."

Zack prodded. "What's right, Maggie?"

A look of irreversible calm stole over her tearstained face. "I want you to step in. Will you adopt my baby?"

The sensation was akin to having a heavyweight's glove belt him in the solar plexus. Zack lost his breath, instantly felt physically ill. At that moment, a waitress with a row of silver studs lining the shell of her left ear appeared at the table.

"You folks want coffee? Breakfast menu'll be out soon if you're hungry."

Trinity said something, Zack didn't hear what. His ears were ringing and he realized he was staring at the baby, looking so tiny and needing someone to rescue her. He'd rescued her once—was it only a week ago? He'd been edgy about that decision. If he'd known how events would play out, would he have left Trinity to sort things out while he'd followed his more basic, less flattering instinct and taken that cab home?

"Zack? Are you all right? Did you hear what Maggie said?"

He pushed back in his seat and the room began to tilt. "Of course I heard." His voice sounded gruff to his own ears and when Maggie recoiled, he summoned up a shaky smile. "Maggie, you do know that Trinity and I... Well, we're not married."

Maggie nodded. "Ms. Cassidy told me. But you're obviously committed to each other." Her hopeful smile shone out. "You're both here, aren't you?"

But, God knows, he hadn't come here for *this*.

"Excuse me a minute." Feeling crowded, Zack fell upon a weak excuse. "I left my cell in the car."

He got to his feet and made his way toward the exit, winding between tables, feeling as if he were moving across the deck of a lilting ship. At the main entry/exit, he put out his palm, crashed through the swinging glass door and out into blessed fresh air. But his stomach was still churning and his legs felt as if they might collapse beneath him. Setting his hands on his knees, he propped himself against the outside brick wall and bent slightly over as his head went into a spin.

He couldn't adopt a baby, not even Bonnie. He was a sworn-to-uphold-the-code bachelor. Cold, hard fact was he didn't have time to worry about a child full time. And Maggie had said she wanted them *both* to adopt. She thought they were committed to each other. Did that mean he was supposed to marry a woman he barely knew? Didn't matter that the woman was Trinity.

He couldn't do it. It might seem like an easy fix for young Maggie, but he was old enough to see on down the line. He wasn't the marrying, settling-down-with-a-brood kind of guy. He'd never professed to be. He was a career man, pure and simple. No blurred lines or people got hurt. This request— the unique situation—changed nothing. And if that sounded harsh, then so be it.

The door swung open. Sucking down another gulp full of fresh air, Zack straightened. Slipping her hands into her coat pockets, Trinity crossed over.

"A bit of a shock, huh?"

He cleared his throat. "Just a bit."

"I think Maggie's really thought this through. She wants to get to know us better. Make a hundred percent sure it's the right thing for the baby."

His head pulled back. "You sound as if you're actually considering this. That it's a done deal."

"If I can help them, I will."

His laugh was clipped. "Well, don't count me in."

She blinked several times. Then a wry, sad grin hooked up one side of the mouth he'd kissed so thoroughly the night before.

"I guess this news has knocked us both out of the ballpark, especially given what I said earlier."

"That we want different things," he reminded her.

She gave a contrite nod. "I'm not sure what it will take to make sure Bel gets everything she deserves. I only know I can't walk away. I truly thought you'd be on board, too. Or would at least consider it." Her beautiful eyes filled. "I honestly thought you loved that little girl."

His jaw clenched. "If I loved her, isn't that all the more reason *not* to set her up like this? I'm not father material."

"You're wrong. You'd make an excellent dad. You're just too stubborn to give up even a smidgen of who you were."

His temper flashed. "Who I *am*."

She folded her arms. "Well, I'm going to help Maggie and Bel."

"With no job?"

"I have savings." Her brows knitted. "Besides, money isn't everything."

"It goes a long way to helping. In fact…" The solution exploded in his head. If he hadn't been so blindsided by Maggie's surprise announcement, he would have thought of it sooner. He couldn't *adopt* but he could certainly help financially.

"I'll transfer money into Maggie's account. As much as she needs."

"So her mother or deadbeat ex can get to it?"

He growled. At times Trinity was so damn difficult. "No. So she can get a place, go to college."

"Who'll look after the baby?"

"Sitters. Even my brothers have sitters."

"I think Maggie is looking at the baby having a stable upbringing, with people who will be there for the long haul rather than a string of girls after a few dollars an hour." She gave him an evaluative, ultimately disapproving look that made him feel about five years old. "I'm going back inside to tell her I'll be there for them both, and if Maggie wants me to take on that child on my own, if there's a way, you can bet I'll do it."

"Trinity, you don't have any support."

That disappointed look turned to jaded pity.

"With that attitude, I think you might be right." She firmed her bottom lip. "That baby's better off without you."

Fourteen

"Mind if I come in?"

With a small smile, Zack shoved his hands in his trouser pockets while Trinity debated with herself whether to slam her apartment's front door in his face. Two weeks had passed since their rescue flight to Colorado, since he'd told her that she wouldn't be able to help Maggie and that baby on her own. She'd brought Maggie and Bel back here to New York anyway and had devised a plan.

It gave her immense pleasure now to say, "As a matter of fact, I do mind. I'm busy."

Looking delectable in black trousers and a white button-down shirt, the cuffs folded up to reveal strong, corded forearms, Zack peered around her. "Packing, I see. You're leaving New York?"

"Heading back to Colorado."

"With Maggie and Bel?"

"She has friends in Denver. There are some great colleges out that way, too."

"Does she know what she wants to study?"

"Domestic law."

"Bet she'll do well." He tipped closer and looked around. "Is she in? I imagine she's been staying here with you."

"She took the baby for a walk."

He tugged an ear. "Do you mind if I come in?"

"You already asked and I already said no."

"I can help you pack."

"I don't need your help."

"Some of those boxes look heavy."

He gave her a hint of his sexy crooked smile but Trinity only glared. His sheepish act wouldn't work. That morning outside of Denver he'd made clear he had his life and no one was going to meddle in it. Well, she had her life, too, and she didn't appreciate it being interrupted now. Still, many times she'd imagined them meeting again, his trying to apologize and her dressing him down. It would be worth a few minutes of her time to make some of the imaginary payback real.

So, with a detached air, she waved him in, shut the door.

"How is Maggie?" he asked while she returned to dismantling her bookshelf.

"Better. We've had a good deal of time to get to know one another. She's an intelligent woman who made a mistake. But when I look at Bel, hear her giggle, I have to be happy that she did."

Zack moved over. Collecting her lone screwdriver from the floor, he began working to take off the top shelf.

"No word from the boyfriend?" he asked.

"He wants nothing to do with either of them." She looked at him pointedly. "He has his own life."

Zack didn't seem to hear her sarcastic note.

She collected a stack of books and fit them in an empty box then pushed to her feet. She'd wanted the chance to show him how she hadn't needed anyone's support, including his. But this was just too awkward. Too painful.

"I really do have a lot to get through."

"I'm helping."

"You're slowing me down."

He set down the screwdriver and stood, too. She'd forgotten how tall he was. He seemed to tower over her. But she wouldn't be intimated. Wouldn't be seduced, either.

He rubbed the back of his neck and admitted, "I behaved badly the other night. I wasn't thinking straight."

"And yet Maggie doesn't have a bad word to say about you. Maybe because she accepts being fobbed off by men." Her father. Her ex. It was a familiar story.

"Or maybe," Zack said, "even in her youth Maggie understood that I needed time."

When he stepped forward, Trinity put up her hands and stepped back. "Maybe I should be as accepting as Maggie but I'm a little touchy right now."

He had the nerve to look contrite and sexy at the same time. "It was a huge thing to get my head around."

"Sometimes a person simply needs to step up and act."

"That's why I'm here."

She made a point of turning her back to reach and remove a painting from the wall. "You'll have to speak to Maggie about any charity you want to offer her."

"I'm not talking about financial support. Well, not exclusively." A heartbeat later she felt his heat close to her back. Heard his deep voice close to her ear. "I'm here to ask you something."

Gathering herself, willing the sudden giddiness away, she purposefully wound around him, painting in hand. "Ask me what?"

"If Bel still needs a father—" he shrugged "—I'm here."

Those words struck her heart as surely as an arrow. He couldn't mean it. He was playing with her emotions. Being cruel.

She growled, "Don't tease, Zack."

"I'm more serious than I've ever been in my life."

She shook her head, certain. "You said you'd never give up who you were." She had a thought. "Unless you're talking about some arrangement…"

He stepped closer. "It's called marriage."

"Marriage?"

"On paper only."

Trinity's heart dropped to her knees. For a moment, she'd held her breath, not daring to believe. For a moment, she'd actually thought…

"You want to help Bel," he said. "So do I. This way we can give her a normal life with a mother and father and all the financial support she needs."

"And you still get to keep your career. Your life."

"It's a win-win."

Her chest began to ache. "And would this marriage include conjugal rights?"

"I was hoping you'd bring that up." His strong arms gathered her near. "I understand about your need to have a family and you understand about my position in the company."

"You mean where your priorities lie."

His brow pinched but then his chin went up. "Precisely." His palms ran down her arms. "What do you say?"

She kept her expression schooled. She would never let him know how much he'd hurt her without even trying. He wanted to marry her. Out of convenience.

She sucked down a breath. "I'm afraid I can't accept."

His dark eyes widened but then he laughed. "Of course you can. This is what you wanted."

Emotion choking her throat, she wound away from him. "It wouldn't do any good to explain."

"Try." He spun her back. "Is it expenses you want to work out? Accommodation? I'll still be working out of New York so you won't have to put up with me all the time."

"And Bel? What kind of a father do you want her to have?"

A frown darkened his eyes. "One who gives a damn."

"You're kidding yourself if you think this can work. How long will it take before you hook up with another starlet or model and find your face splashed over the tabloids again? You were right. You are what you are. And Bel deserves better...." She lifted her chin. "I do, too."

He thought he'd offered a solution but he'd only insulted her. She and Bel were worthy of respect. Of love and real commitment. But he obviously didn't see that.

Tears filling her eyes, she crossed to the door and opened it wide.

"You need to go, Zack, and, please, do us all a favor and never come back."

Fifteen

"I was surprised to hear you weren't in the office today. Anything wrong?"

Zack had opened his door to find his father waiting. Without his usual untroubled smile, he stepped aside. "Just wasn't feeling so hot."

"You haven't taken a day off in the whole time you've worked at the company." His father stepped inside. "Maybe I should call a doctor."

"I just needed some time…to think."

Zack moved across the lounge room, out onto the balcony, his father right behind.

"Does this have anything to do with that young lady you were besotted with at your sister's engagement party?"

Zack sat down at the outdoor setting. "I looked besotted?"

"At one stage, I wondered whether I was going to have to announce a second Harrison betrothal that night."

Since seeing Trinity again, Zack thought he'd done a great job keeping his frustration, hurt, guilt, need, under control. He'd had so many short-term affairs, frankly, he'd lost count. Parting was never the highlight of any relationship, but he couldn't recall ever having been involved long enough or deeply enough to suffer untowardly when the curtain had dropped.

Trinity was right. He was stubborn. And selfish. Intimate companionships without the demands and responsibilities had suited him down to the ground. But she was a hundred times different. A thousand. If she wasn't he wouldn't have asked her to marry him. He wanted to support them both, Trinity and the baby. And she'd told him to leave and never come back. God help him, she'd meant it, too.

He'd lost the only woman he'd ever really cared about and the finality in that truth was nearly driving him mad.

"I can't see her again," Zack growled as his father pulled up a chair, too.

"Although it's evident you want to very much."

Zack declined to answer. Rather, he simply gazed out over the view, imagining families enjoying Central Park on a perfect spring day, and then he wondered where Trinity and the baby were now. Whether they missed him like he missed them. But what more could he do?

His chest tightened, he clamped shut his eyes and groaned.

What the hell did she want from him?

After a time, his father spoke. "The heart's a funny thing. There are some mighty powerful forces in this world of ours, but love beats them all, hands down."

Zack frowned across. "Are you trying to say that you still love Mom?"

"Even if she decides it's time to call it a day, I'll never regret marrying her, having our family together." He ran a finger over his graying moustache. "I'm not so young anymore. You begin to see life through a different lens when you hit sixty. Your ideas regarding success change. Some of the loneliest people in the world have bursting bank accounts." He looked down and nodded to himself. "I often wonder where I'd be now if I hadn't fallen so in love with your mother. I might have spent too much time away, but I was always so grateful to come home to you all. Birthdays, Christmas, all those great vacations in Colorado. Remember that old barn we spent that god-awful night in?"

Zack summoned up a smile. "I'll never forget it."

"When you're counting down rather than building up, those are the times that matter, not whether or not you beat down some poor bastard in a takeover bid."

Zack sat forward. "Were you ever afraid of becoming a father? The responsibilities, I mean."

"Don't know a man who isn't. Just goes to show you're not about to take the role lightly. Every child deserves that consideration. But if a man is fortunate enough to find his soul mate, in my opinion, he'd be a fool not to grab the whole package with open arms."

"What if you screw up?"

"Work damn hard to make sure you don't."

Zack swallowed against the hollow feeling rising in his gut. "No matter how hard I work, Trinity won't want to see me again."

When his father sat back and thatched fingers on his lap, preparing to listen, Zack surprised himself and let the whole story out, including his offer of marriage.

"I've seen her angry at me, frustrated, but seeing the disappointment in her eyes that day just about killed me."

"It's not something that can be mended?" his father asked.

"I don't see how."

"Maybe the family needs to throw another engagement party soon."

Zack tried not to sound annoyed. "Dad, I told you she's not interested."

"Perhaps you didn't ask her the right way." His father got to his feet. "You were always so sure of yourself and that largely has to do with instinct." He clasped his son's shoulder and squeezed. "Surrender to your instincts now and you might end up scoring the deal of your life."

Sixteen

Trinity was heading back inside after making sure Maggie had caught her lift into town safely, when something odd caught her eye. Something small, round and clear glinting in the sunshine in the garden.

She, Maggie and the baby had moved back to Denver two weeks ago and there was still plenty to do to make this single-story three-bedroom rental feel more like a home. The walls longed for a fresh coat of paint, the furniture needed updating and the yard couldn't wait for leaves to be raked and some bright spring blooms to be planted. Remembering Mrs. Dale, Trinity had thought dianthus. She planned to start gardening this weekend.

But with her foot on the first porch step, she wondered if she ought to start on that tidying now. Bel was asleep in the front room and it was such a gorgeous morning. So different than the day she and Bel had first met. The day dynamo Zack Harrison had blown in to her life.

And had blown right out again, Trinity reminded herself

as she headed for that curious spot in the garden. She wondered how many other women would turn down the chance to be Zack's wife, even when the marriage was purely for show. Sometimes, when she felt lonely and wondered if tossing out her old life for a new one was totally insane, she'd think about how pleased he'd looked after offering what he must have believed to be a very attractive out for her.

Chivalrous in his own way, she supposed, as that glint caught her eye again. Maybe if she hadn't cared so much—if she hadn't fallen in love—she might have accepted the deal for the baby's sake. Had she been selfish in refusing his proposal? Should she have thought of Bel first and her own feelings not at all?

But those doubts never lasted long. In her heart she knew what that child—any child—needed most. Not money or a person to call *daddy* whenever he could slot in a visit and jet into town. Trinity also knew what she needed. She might not have felt loved growing up but now she was grown—now she had a say and a choice—she wouldn't settle for anything less than the real deal.

Kneeling in the garden now, she brushed away the dried leaves built up around that piece of glinting glass and, in a heartbeat, reality seemed to turn in on itself. Scooping the piece up, she examined it from every angle while her stomach pitched and her thoughts began to fly.

This wasn't a random piece of glass. She'd found a replica of the snow globe Zack had given her. Only the scene inside this one was different. A man and woman stood side by side, a groom and his bride. They were waiting outside a chapel. A message was engraved on the gold plaque.

Marry Me.

Taken aback, Trinity fell sideways and almost dropped the globe. Zack had been here, had left this. But when? How? What was she supposed to think, to do, to say?

"You found my surprise."

At the familiar deep tones, Trinity swung around. Zack stood an arm's length away wearing blue jeans and a sexy white T-shirt. She tried to speak but her mind was whirling too fast. Surprise, affront, even wild, silly hope, were barraging her from every angle. Zack took pity on her.

"I should explain," he said.

Shaky, she held up the globe. "If this is some sick way of tabling that marriage of convenience again, the answer's still no."

"Haven't lost that temper, I see."

"Don't turn this around. Zack, I asked you to leave us alone." To let her heal. To forget.

Not only did he ignore that. He moved closer.

"I heard from Mrs. Dale this morning," he said. "They're moving into a retirement apartment. She wondered if I knew a good home for Cruiser. I said I did."

An image of that big, beautiful hound flashed to the forefront of her mind and Trinity smiled. "Who?"

"Me."

"You're going to take Cruiser to New York?"

"As it turns out, no. I also spoke with James Dirkins recently. Hope you don't mind but I put your offer to him. I asked whether he'd consider being my partner in owning and running his hotel. Took him two seconds to agree. Said it was the perfect solution and he's very much looking forward to working with me." His expression sobered. "Seems I remind him of his son."

"I'm happy for him." She truly was. "But how does that tie in with Cruiser. Does Mr. Dirkins want a dog?"

"Cruiser will be staying with me. I'm moving here, permanently." While she stared in stunned disbelief, he slipped the globe from her hand. "Which brings us to this."

When he shook the globe and snow rained down on the happy scene, she brought herself back.

"No, Zack. I said no."

"You haven't heard me out."

"I don't need to. I'm not going to be anyone's convenience. Maggie, Bel and I will do fine on our own. Kate's given me freelance work editing for *Story*—jobs I can do from here. And I have two other publications interested in the same type of thing."

But Zack seemed to be only half listening. Rather he was busy unscrewing the globe's base. From a secret compartment, he slid out a ring…a beautiful stone the color of her eyes surrounded by a ring of sparkling diamonds. Her head began to swim.

This was too much.

Trinity shook her head slowly, tried to back away. "This isn't fair."

He reached for her hand. "I'm talking about a marriage based on mutual respect. A union, Trinity, based on love. My love for you and yours for me." His dark eyes burned into hers. "I want you to be my bride. And I'd want that whether there was a beautiful baby needing us or not."

For a short, sweet moment, the words sang around in her head. He wanted them to be married—for real. But it didn't make sense. Not after all he'd said and explained about a career-first mind-set getting in the way of a sound marriage. And didn't his parents' rocky marriage support that claim?

"You as good as said yourself. When a man takes his work as a mistress, sooner or later resentment sinks in. If you want the best for Bel, if you really love me—"

"I really do."

"—then you'd walk away now. Bel needs stability."

He nodded as if he understood. "I've told my father and the rest of the mob, I'm stepping down from the role of chairman-in-waiting. In fact, I offered my resignation from the family board."

Trinity blinked as the words hit then sank in. That couldn't be. "But you are Harrison Hotels."

"Was. Now I'm Bel's future father. Your future husband. That is, if you say yes."

"Zack, this is crazy. You need to think this through."

"I've done nothing but think. Now it's time to act." He

wound an arm around her waist and pressed her near. "I love you, and that's a thousand times more important than wheeling and dealing. Turns out I'm exactly like my brothers. I want to settle down. Have a family." He dropped a kiss on the side of her mouth. "I want that with you. Only you."

She breathed out a question. "And Bel?"

"She'll be the jewel in our crown. The happy ending to our story."

Trinity felt her eyes prickle and fill. All at once, she felt so happy. Bubbling and wanting to cry with it. A happy ending. She siphoned down a breath then said, "I've always wanted one of those."

"I know what I want. You."

"Are you sure?"

He grinned. "I'm so sure, it's scary."

Her heart was pounding so hard, and she didn't feel as if she could get enough air. She couldn't believe it. "You really love me?"

"Until the day I die."

That happy sob building in her throat finally escaped over a heartfelt smile. Suddenly she felt so full she wondered if she might burst.

"I didn't want to tell you..."

"Tell me what?"

She surrendered. "That I love you, too." Hopelessly and with all her heart. It had killed her to tell him to leave that day. She never thought she'd see him again.

He was slipping the ring on her finger, bringing her hand to his lips and, as tears spilled down her cheeks, for the first time in her life Trinity felt truly whole.

When he gathered her close, she had to say, "I just hope you don't miss any of your old life."

"Not a chance," he said.

And a heartbeat before his mouth covered hers, in love's sweetest words, he told her why.

Epilogue

Nine months later

Surrounded by a sea of smiling faces, Trinity felt like a princess standing beside the man who had stolen and would always keep her heart. As they cut through the bottom tier of their soaring wedding cake and enthusiastic applause went up in the Denver Dirkins-Harrison Hotel ballroom, she let out a laugh of sheer joy and lifted her face to accept a kiss from the handsome groom. Although they'd planned this special day for months, brimming with emotion now, Trinity couldn't quite believe this dream had come true.

When the applause and flashes finally died, looking dynamic in his tuxedo, his dark hair combed back and onyx eyes sparkling, Zack broke the kiss but stayed close to murmur against her cheek.

"Are you tired of smiling for the cameras yet?"

She snatched a kiss from his strong jaw, drank in his familiar masculine scent and confessed, "I don't think I'll *ever* stop smiling."

Today she'd not only said "I do" to the most wonderful man on the planet, she'd also been formally welcomed into his family. She'd almost cried she'd been so moved by Dylan's speech announcing how pleased all the Harrisons were to have her join their fold. Zack's parents and siblings, in-laws and their children had also welcomed in another lucky person, a beautiful shining soul she and Zack fell more in love with each and every day.

Since their attorney had finalized the open adoption, Belinda—or Bonnie Bell as she'd become known—had stayed full-time with them in their Colorado cabin. But Maggie was welcome whenever and as often as she pleased. They never wanted their baby girl to forget her biological mother—a young woman who grew stronger every day and was doing so well, via Harrison sponsorship, at a nearby college studying law.

Maggie had been invited today, but casting a quick glance over their guests now, Trinity couldn't spot either Maggie or Bel. Zack must have read her look.

"There's Maggie." Zack gestured to the wedding gift table where Maggie was speaking with Sienna, who had been thrilled to be a bridesmaid. "But I can't see the baby."

"You look down that way and I'll take this end."

Before she could shoot off, he cupped her bare shoulders and peered patiently into her eyes.

"Honey, we're among friends and family. Not to mention security personnel manning the exits." A gate-crasher measure more than anything. "I'm sure someone has Bonnie at their table, telling her how pretty she is as she totters around on those new little shoes she loves."

Trinity nodded and found a smile. "Guess I'm feeling a little anxious—" *guilty* "—over leaving her for a whole week for our honeymoon in Italy."

"She'll be with Maggie and my mother, too." He lifted her hand and dropped a tender kiss on the sensitive underside of her wrist. "She'll be so spoiled we'll have to put her in baby boot camp when we get back."

Trinity laughed but couldn't pretend she didn't already feel that "something missing" sensation, the one she'd first experienced the second day they'd spent cut off from the rest of the world in his cabin. The unease must have shown on her face.

He brought her hands folded in his to his chest. "Trin, you haven't got a neglectful bone in your body. You're an amazing mom. That little girl's face lights up whenever you're around."

Trinity melted. "She's pretty fond of you, too."

The music faded at the same time MC Dylan clicked on the mic to make an announcement. It was time for the bridal waltz.

The lights went down and a show of slow, spinning lights rotated around the floor as the twelve-piece band kicked off a moving song they'd both chosen. Their audience sighed as he took her in his arms and, with expert skill, moved her around beneath the "stars."

With everyone watching, but for her ears only, Zack said, "I thank my lucky stars you jumped into my cab that day and found us." Trinity's breath caught high in her chest at the depth of feeling shining in those intelligent dark eyes. "I can't bear to think of never having met you, of missing out on knowing and loving you both. I'll miss Bel, too, when we're on our honeymoon, but a week will fly by."

"And next vacation, we'll take her."

"This time Italy. Next vacation, what about Disney World?"

Her heart leaped. "Oh, Bonnie will love it!" So would she.

He laughed. "Disney World it is."

Without warning, he caught her waist and, next minute, her feet were off the ground and her voluminous fairy-tale skirt whooshed out as he spun her around. The crowd clapped and more flashes went off before he set her gently down and his focus shifted.

"There she is."

Trinity looked over her shoulder. The baby was sitting on

her grandfather's hip, studying him solemnly as she pulled his moustache and he talked, probably passing on some Harrison family story. Zack's mother joined the pair. She said something to them both, pointed to the dance floor, and all three laughed and group hugged. Trinity's heart swelled to double its size. Bel couldn't have wished for better grandparents.

"I'm glad your parents have worked out their differences," she said as they continued to dance and other couples began to join in.

"Dad always said that for any venture to succeed you must be prepared to weather the storms. After all these years of hard slog, my mother wanted some time with him. It was hard to let go and give up what he'd worked his whole life to achieve."

"But he hasn't given it up. He's passed it on."

"An equal share to all his children with each sibling having an equal say in decisions."

"Do you ever feel cheated? I mean you wanted to be the sole chairman of Harrison Hotels for so long."

"I feel only blessed." His palm ironed up the back of her gown as he urged her closer still. "The worst time of my life was when I thought I'd lost you. Anything to do with the company pales in comparison. I intend to spend the rest of my life making certain we stay as happy as we are tonight. I want to wake up to your beautiful, smiling face every morning for the next fifty or sixty years, until we're confined to wheelchairs, content to watch our hoards of great-grandchildren grow up."

She blinked back happy tears enough to ask, "Are you saying...?"

"We'll discuss it later, when we're alone and can invest some quality time in pursuing the matter of expanding our family."

Trinity's step faltered and she tramped on his foot. Had she understood right? They'd had hypothetical discussions but hadn't made any firm decision, as far as she knew.

His gaze on her lips, he curved a fingertip around her cheek and chin. "You still want to try for a baby, don't you, honey?"

Tears filled her eyes, clogged her throat. Her reply was husky, trembling. Overjoyed!

"Zack, I've never wanted anything more in my life. I want Bel to have brothers and sisters." The wish was so strong, she felt *weak* with the hope.

"Then let's get started." He nudged his chin one brother's way. "Mason's got three and one on the way. Reckon we can top that?"

"I'd like to try."

As they laughed and spun around on the floor, Trinity concentrated to remember every detail and then lock this instant of pure perfection away in her heart forever. Those moments were building up and she knew there'd be so many more.

"You're the most beautiful bride that's ever been," he told her. "I can't believe how lucky I am."

"I wonder if you'll think that when those 3:00 a.m. feedings come around."

"I'm looking forward to it, the same way I'm looking forward to every minute of our lives together."

Never more content, she drank in the handsome, strong lines of his face. "How is it that every single day there's something more to love about you?"

Zack looked at her with only devotion and delight in his eyes and then his head lowered and his wonderful smile covered hers.

As Trinity gave herself over to the sparks flying through her blood and dreams of tomorrow forming in her head, for a heartbeat she remembered how dark her existence had once been a long time ago. But she'd weathered each day and each fateful step had led her to this phenomenal present...to a wonderful husband, beautiful child and fabulous future she couldn't wait to meet.

* * * * *

REQUEST YOUR FREE BOOKS!
2 FREE NOVELS PLUS 2 FREE GIFTS!

♦ Harlequin®

Desire

ALWAYS POWERFUL, PASSIONATE AND PROVOCATIVE

YES! Please send me 2 FREE Harlequin Desire® novels and my 2 FREE gifts (gifts are worth about $10). After receiving them, if I don't wish to receive any more books, I can return the shipping statement marked "cancel." If I don't cancel, I will receive 6 brand-new novels every month and be billed just $4.30 per book in the U.S. or $4.99 per book in Canada. That's a saving of at least 14% off the cover price! It's quite a bargain! Shipping and handling is just 50¢ per book in the U.S. and 75¢ per book in Canada.* I understand that accepting the 2 free books and gifts places me under no obligation to buy anything. I can always return a shipment and cancel at any time. Even if I never buy another book, the two free books and gifts are mine to keep forever.

225/326 HDN FEF3

Name	(PLEASE PRINT)	
Address		Apt. #
City	State/Prov.	Zip/Postal Code

Signature (if under 18, a parent or guardian must sign)

Mail to the **Reader Service:**
IN U.S.A.: P.O. Box 1867, Buffalo, NY 14240-1867
IN CANADA: P.O. Box 609, Fort Erie, Ontario L2A 5X3

Not valid for current subscribers to Harlequin Desire books.

Want to try two free books from another line?
Call 1-800-873-8635 or visit www.ReaderService.com.

* Terms and prices subject to change without notice. Prices do not include applicable taxes. Sales tax applicable in N.Y. Canadian residents will be charged applicable taxes. Offer not valid in Quebec. This offer is limited to one order per household. All orders subject to credit approval. Credit or debit balances in a customer's account(s) may be offset by any other outstanding balance owed by or to the customer. Please allow 4 to 6 weeks for delivery. Offer available while quantities last.

Your Privacy—The Reader Service is committed to protecting your privacy. Our Privacy Policy is available online at www.ReaderService.com or upon request from the Reader Service.

We make a portion of our mailing list available to reputable third parties that offer products we believe may interest you. If you prefer that we not exchange your name with third parties, or if you wish to clarify or modify your communication preferences, please visit us at www.ReaderService.com/consumerchoice or write to us at Reader Service Preference Service, P.O. Box 9062, Buffalo, NY 14269. Include your complete name and address.

HDES11B

Montana. Home of big blue skies, wide open spaces...and really hot men! Join bestselling author Debbi Rawlins in celebrating all things Western in Harlequin® Blaze™ with her new miniseries, MADE IN MONTANA!

Read on for a sneak peek of
BAREFOOT BLUE JEAN NIGHT

"OVER HERE," Cole said.

Jamie headed toward him, her lips rising in a cheeky grin. "What makes you think I'm looking for you?"

He drew her back into the shadows inside the barn. "Then tell me, Jamie, what are you looking for?"

A spark had ignited between them and she had the distinct feeling that tonight was the night for fireworks—despite the threat of thieves. The only unanswered question was when.

"Oh, I get it," she said finally. "You're trying to distract me from telling you I'm going to help you keep watch."

He lowered both hands. "No, you're not."

"I am. Rachel thinks it's an excellent idea."

He shot a frown toward the kitchen. "I don't care what my sister thinks. You have five minutes, then you're marching right back into that house."

She wasn't about to let him get away with pulling back. Not to mention she didn't care for his bossiness. "You're such a coward."

"Let's put it this way..." He arched a brow. "How much watching do you think we'd get done?"

She flattened a palm on his chest. His heart pounded as hard as hers. "I see your point. But no, I won't be a good little girl and do as you so charmingly ordered."

"It wasn't an order," he muttered. "It was a strongly

worded request. I have to stay alert out here."

"Correct. That's why we'll behave like adults and refrain from making out."

"Making out," he repeated with a snort. "Haven't heard that term in a while." Then he caught her wrist and pulled her hand away from his chest. "Not a good start."

"It's barely dark. No one's going to sneak in now. Once we seriously need to pay attention, I'll be as good as gold. But I figure we have at least an hour."

"For?"

"Oh, I don't know…" With the tip of her finger she traced his lower lip. "Nothing too risky. Just some kissing. Maybe I'll even let you get to first base."

Cole laughed. "Honey, I've never stopped at first base before and I'm not about to start now."

Don't miss BAREFOOT BLUE JEAN NIGHT
by Debbi Rawlins.

Available August 2012 from Harlequin® Blaze™
wherever books are sold.